D0049086

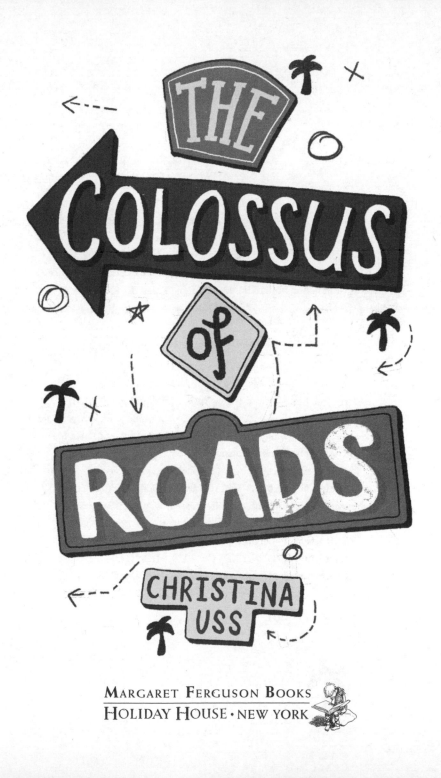

THE COLOSSUS of ROADS

CHRISTINA USS

MARGARET FERGUSON BOOKS
HOLIDAY HOUSE · NEW YORK

Margaret Ferguson Books
Copyright © 2020 by Christina Uss
All rights reserved
HOLIDAY HOUSE is registered in the U.S. Patent and Trademark Office.
Printed and bound in March 2020 at Maple Press, York, PA, U.S.A.
First Edition
1 3 5 7 9 10 8 6 4 2
Library of Congress Cataloging-in-Publication Data

Names: Uss, Christina, author.
Title: The Colossus of Roads / Christina Uss.
Description: First edition. | New York : Holiday House, [2020]
Audience: Ages 9–12. | Audience: Grades 5–6. | Summary: Eleven-year-old
Rick Rusek, nearly homebound by motion sickness, wants to help his
family's catering business by unsnarling Los Angeles traffic, but first
he must help a Girl Scout troop with an art project.
Identifiers: LCCN 2019025604 | ISBN 9780823444502 (hardcover)
Subjects: CYAC: Family life—California—Los Angeles—Fiction.
Traffic congestion—Fiction. | Motion sickness—Fiction. | Scouting
(Youth activity)—Fiction. | Los Angeles (Calif.)—Fiction.
Classification: LCC PZ7.1.U86 Col 2020 | DDC [Fic]—dc23
LC record available at https://lccn.loc.gov/2019025604

To kids in backseats everywhere, who wonder
if their talents matter

----> CONTENTS <----

CHEESEBURGERS! YES!

RICK RUSEK'S STOMACH grumbled, trying to get his attention. He ignored it and sat back on his heels, gazing at the rectangle of heavy-gauge aluminum on his bedroom floor. The sign looked a lot better now that he'd swabbed it in the bathtub with some wet paper towels. He admired its clean lines, black words bold and solid against the candy-corn-orange background:

ROAD WORK NEXT 5 MILES

It was Wednesday night, and his radio played the all-weather all-traffic station on low volume. He listened with half an ear to reports of cars clogging Los Angeles freeways and desert winds sweeping toward the Pacific Ocean.

Rick had never been to the beach, even though the California coast was only thirty miles from his home, but the constant noise of cars driving by outside his window was what he imagined ocean waves sounded like. That is, if the ocean's rhythmic *whoosh-shoosh* got punctuated by the occasional shark on a thundering motorcycle, or by dolphins booming bass-heavy hip-hop.

He flipped the sign over and studied the back. A two-foot-long chunk of the metal pole that had originally held it up was still attached with thick, rusty nuts and bolts. Rick carefully ran a finger over the ridges of one bolt. Once upon a time, all these bits of steel had been shiny and the sign had been new. "How long has it been since you've gotten to do your job, sign?" he murmured. "I bet you didn't like lying in the dirt instead of telling cars what's coming."

The squeak and groan of the front door opening startled Rick out of his one-sided conversation. He shot a glance at the clock. Dad was the latest he'd ever been. Rick usually stayed with his next-door neighbors, the Herreras, after school, until Mom or Dad came to get him. Their town house shared a wall with his town house. But the Herreras had plans that evening, so when his dad had called to let them know he was going to be late, he'd told Rick to walk home, lock the door, and wait. He'd suggested that since Rick was eleven now, it could be considered one of his trial runs of Pre-Teen Responsibility, a phrase both parents had been using a lot lately. Rick had taken a slight detour to collect the sign from an empty lot near his house.

Dinner! Rick's stomach burbled. *Finally!*

"I'm home!" his father called. The sound of steps and jingling car keys headed toward the kitchenette.

"In my room, Dad!" Rick replied, standing up. The steps and jingling moved upstairs and became a knock and a turning doorknob.

"Hey there." Dad came in and gave Rick a one-armed hug, his scruffy sideburns rubbing against Rick's ear. "Sorry I didn't get home sooner, but it was a rough day to drive the Five." "The Five," short for the 5 Freeway, was one of a dozen long, slow-moving freeways that could turn nightmarish at rush hour. Rick's mom and dad ran a catering business delivering gourmet Polish food around Los Angeles. Navigating traffic was as much a part of their job as cooking tasty food. "The traffic made us late setting up a lunch buffet, then late delivering for a dinner event. Mom's still finishing the prep work for tomorrow's cooking. She'll be home with the delivery van . . . oh, sometime before next week, if we're lucky."

Dad noticed the ROAD WORK sign amid the shorts and socks on the floor. "Found something else? Kiddo, Mom's not going to be impressed with your level of Pre-Teen Responsibility when you're bringing home more roadside junk."

"Dad, this is not roadside junk," Rick said, turning the sign right-side up. Bringing this home was nothing like bringing the broken traffic light lens he'd found last week. "This is a high-intensity prismatic sign with corrosion-resistant engineering-grade metal and everything. It needed someone to care about it."

"And that just had to be you, huh?" Dad sat down

heavily on Rick's bed. "Well, maybe you can tell me more while we have some dinner. Oh no, dinner!" Dad groaned and rubbed his eyes with the palms of both hands. "I was supposed to stop by the supermarket on the way home. We haven't got anything in the house to eat except left-over cabbage rolls. I don't think I can even look at another cabbage roll."

"They wouldn't be my first choice, either," said Rick. Mom and Dad's catering business was called Smotch, the first syllable from the Polish word *Smacznego*, which means "Enjoy your meal!" in Polish, like *Bon appétit* does in French. (Mom explained that *smacz* rhymed with *watch* and *nego* rhymed with *Lego* to non–Polish speakers.) Mom had started the business five years ago, and it was a hit. She was known for the wonderful meals she made from scratch and delivered the same day she prepared them. Soon she had so many orders, she rented space in an industrial kitchen in their neighborhood. Dad had decided to quit working as a graphic designer to help her prepare and deliver her kielbasas (smoked sausages), pierogi (pasta pockets filled with everything from pota-toes and cheese to blueberries), cabbage rolls stuffed with meat and rice, creamy mushrooms, cucumber salad, spicy horseradish sauce, and especially her soft rye bread.

Los Angeles was a big place, spanning five hundred square miles. Mom and Dad fed hungry folks all over the area, from their not-so-fancy suburb in the arid San Fernando Valley to swanky places like Beverly Hills and

Marina del Rey. With so much time spent cooking and driving, the Rusek family often ended up eating leftovers. None of them liked eating Polish food anywhere near as much as they had before the business took off.

"What'll we do? We don't even have bread or eggs," Dad said. "Pretty sure we have some canned beets . . . or . . ." He trailed off, looking at Rick's walls as if some appetizing inspiration might jump out. "Say, did you put up some more maps?"

"Yep," Rick said proudly. "Figured out a bunch more ways to fix traffic patterns." Over the past few years, he'd thumbtacked dozens of multicolored map pages from a spiral-bound LA street atlas to his walls. Under each map he'd taped a piece of graph paper filled with precisely penciled grids, arrows, and measurements. He called these his Snarl Solutions, his unique ideas about how to improve traffic flow. Rick tried hard to make them look like they'd been crafted by a professional traffic engineer.

It was the most fun hobby: he'd trace a route on a map from his atlas, then use his computer to examine it up close on Google Street View, where a few clicks of his mouse allowed him to spin in 360 degrees as if he were standing in the middle of any street or freeway in the city. (His second-grade teacher had introduced Rick and the other students to this online tool so they could "visit" neighborhoods in countries like Mexico, Germany, and South Korea.) Rick traveled the streets of LA from the comfort of his bedroom, saw what road signs were already there, and then recorded his ideas on how they could be better. He had the sense that little changes, like lowering or increasing the speed limit or shifting the location of a sign by a couple of feet so drivers could see it sooner, would have a big impact. Too bad he'd never been able to see if his theories worked.

"Huh. I guess it's like wallpaper telling our family history through streets and freeways," Dad mused. The few places Rick had been driven to in LA, plus every place his parents had delivered food, were on these walls. Since he was six, he and his dad had sat down at the dining room table to map out the best route to every new delivery location. Rick wished he could be as useful as his much-older twin brothers, Aleks and Thomas, who'd helped with cooking, delivering, serving, plus watching Rick, before they'd moved out last year to attend college, but Dad insisted Rick's contribution was just as important. Both brothers were studying at UCLA, living in the dorms and working on-campus jobs, so they were too busy to visit home often.

"There's just something about printed maps," his dad was saying now. "You can trust a paper map. They don't print it unless they're sure it's right. Our darn GPS always wants me to turn right into people's houses or turn left off cliffs." Ignoring the graph-paper grids, he pointed to one map. "I remember here in Hollywood when we catered the premiere for that movie about Marie Curie. And this map shows city hall, where the palm trees dropped fronds into the bowl of mushrooms. And here's your old school. The Ruseks—a family history measured in mileage!" He stood studying the maps until Rick's stomach let out a loud growl: *Forgetting dinner?*

Dad rubbed his eyes again. "What would you eat right now if you could?"

"Anything but cabbage rolls, really," Rick said. His stomach gurgled in 100 percent agreement.

"If only I could teleport us to In-N-Out Burger for Double-Double cheeseburgers," his dad said dreamily.

Cheeseburgers! Rick's stomach called out. *Yes! Let's go now!*

"Cheeseburgers! Yes! Let's go now!" Rick repeated without thinking.

Dad grimaced and said, "Oh, kiddo." Rick knew that meant no. Rick's motion sickness had ruled his family's life since he was a toddler. No medication had yet been able to cure it, so his parents drove him places only when it was strictly necessary. His family knew every restaurant within a four-mile radius that offered delivery, but they never ate at them in person. (Rick's new gastroenterologist had called his nausea "intervention-resistant" and half-jokingly recommended they consider moving to a city with no cars, like Venice, Italy. "But don't they use boats there?" Mom had wailed. "What about seasickness?")

In-N-Out did not deliver. "Maybe I should pick up an order and bring it home?" Dad said without enthusiasm.

"Too bad takeout doesn't do In-N-Out's food justice." The drive there and back was long enough that burgers arrived home cold, congealed, and sad. "Nah, let's forget cheeseburgers and order Chinese." He scrolled through his contacts on his phone and tapped the number. "Delivery, please. What? That's too long a wait for us, thanks anyway." He tried the Indian place and found out their delivery person's car had broken down. Then he called the Pizza Shoppe. "Hello? Yes, we'd like a large half-pepperoni, half-pineapple for delivery. How long will it take?" Dad mouthed *an hour and a half* at Rick while rolling his eyes. "I guess it is what it is," he said, giving their address.

After he hung up, Rick and Dad shared a hungry, disappointed look. Dad said, "I can't believe how busy these places are in the middle of the week."

"Maybe you could call Mom and ask her to bring something home?" Rick suggested.

Dad shook his head. "It's been such a tough day for both of us, I don't want to ask her to do one more thing. Besides, she might not get here any earlier than the pizza."

Usually, Rick's stomach encouraged staying home and waiting for delivery, but tonight it was acting strange. It started repeating *cheeseburgers cheeseburgers cheeseburgers* like a sacred chant.

There's no way, Rick told it. *Shush.*

His stomach paused its chanting and said, *But cheeseburgers. Maybe try the breathing thing?* The gastroenterologist had given Rick a deep-breathing technique that she said might help. Rick had been to a lot of doctors, and this new one had some pretty odd ideas.

If his stomach was game, Rick was willing. "Dad—what if we don't give up on In-N-Out that easily? Remember the deep-breathing exercise the doctor suggested? I can give it a shot," he said.

Dad perked up. "Do you think it could work?" Rick could see parental concern fighting with burger cravings on his father's face.

"We won't know until we try," Rick said. He dug out the paper from the doctor describing what to do from his desk drawer. "And if it does, cheeseburgers."

CHEESEBURGERS! his stomach shouted.

Dad took Rick's right hand in both of his own and shook it solemnly. "You're a brave young man. And I'm a hungry dad. And like you said, we won't know until we try." Dad called to cancel the pizza and they headed downstairs to the carport.

Rick opened the back door of his dad's old Jeep, repeating the breathing sequence to himself under his breath. *In-two-three-four, hold-two-three-four, out-two-three-four.* He was supposed to pinch closed alternating nostrils on the ins and outs. It was complicated.

Dad smiled nervously into the rearview mirror and turned on the ignition. "Right. We're doing this. Seize the day."

The car reversed onto Foothill Boulevard. Rick rolled his window halfway down and breathed in to the count of four. He kept doggedly breathing and counting, but at the first intersection, he had to grab a double-reinforced airsickness bag from the thick wad tucked into the seat pocket in front of him. His parents ordered them in bulk on the internet.

Why are you breathing so slowly? his stomach blorped at him. *Is this the breathing exercise? Need more oxygen! Not going to make it!* Then it made a sound like a herd of unhappy moose bellowing *Nooooo.*

Rick ditched the exercises, gulped in air, and started focusing his attention out the window as hard as he could on the street signs and how the cars around them were driving. He invited his mind to try to solve traffic puzzles instead of worrying over the disastrous things happening inside his body. His dad looked at him in the rearview mirror and pulled into a hardware store parking lot nowhere near their destination.

"This was a mistake," Dad said. "We're going to park here until you feel better, and then we're going back home."

Rick didn't respond because he couldn't. While they waited, his dad called the Pizza Shoppe to reinstate their order. Once his stomach had quieted somewhat, he signaled Dad in the rearview mirror. Dad pulled out carefully and Rick concentrated extra-hard on the road signs, begging his digestive system to give him a break.

I can't help my gut reactions, his stomach argued. *Your part of the deal is not to put me in these situations.*

You were the one chanting about cheeseburgers! Rick answered. *You said we should try the breathing techniques!*

You know I'm an organ of your body and I only talk in your imagination, right? his stomach said. *My bad choices belong to both of us.*

Back home, Rick crawled onto the couch and whimpered. Dad laid a cool, wet washcloth across his forehead and placed a cup of water from the kitchen sink within Rick's reach. "What was I thinking?" he said. "I'm so sorry. Guess deep breathing is yet another cure that doesn't work for you."

Rick waved vaguely.

Dad said, "Maybe we don't tell your mother about this? She'd kill me."

Rick gave him a thumbs-up. If he could help it, he didn't want more than one parent hovering over him. He lay in ruins for a while. When he was ready to speak, he croaked, "Can you tell me about the traffic problems you had on the way home?"

"Oh, son, how about we leave traffic discussions for another day?" Dad said, taking a container of cabbage rolls out of the refrigerator. He stuck his tongue out at them and slid them back into the fridge.

Rick reluctantly pulled his mind away from the tantalizing riddle of his dad's drive home. Dad always said he appreciated Rick's help with mapping delivery routes, but both he and especially Mom treated Rick's passion for studying traffic patterns as a strange phase Rick was bound to outgrow, like when he'd insisted on wearing a Spider-Man mask to bed.

Understanding traffic wasn't the same as loving a Spider-Man mask. Rick distinctly remembered when he'd started getting carsick on the way to day care near Dad's work as a little kid. Even before he could recite his ABCs without forgetting the whole section between *Q* and *W*, he understood that the road signs said important things that made a difference to how the cars moved. Staring out the window to study the cars and signs took his mind off the nausea.

That was when we started talking, his stomach reminded him. Rick told his stomach how he thought different road signs might make the traffic move better. Having those conversations seemed to calm it down. *And one time, I said maybe you'd been bitten by a radioactive spider and this was your resulting superpower. And then you wore your Spider-Man mask to bed every night*, his stomach added. Okay, so the two things were related. But he'd outgrown one. The other one grew with him, like his skin.

"Tell me about the new school," his dad said. "Are you finding the work challenging enough?" Both Dad and Mom were worried that the school Rick had transferred to for fifth grade might be crummy.

"Sure. Plenty of challenges," Rick answered.

"Like . . . ?" Dad prompted.

Rick said, "Ummmmm . . ." Eleanor Roosevelt Elementary's most striking feature was how every hallway was plastered with quotes from famous people exhorting the students to reach higher, believe harder, and never give up on anything. "The art teacher has a museum curator coming to talk to us tomorrow." He propped himself on his elbows and sipped some water while he tried to think of something else to say. His stomach questioned whether it wanted any water yet. His face must have shown it, because his dad winced.

Dad took the cup from Rick and sat down next to him on the couch. "Someday, son. Someday this won't be a challenge for you. And on that day, we'll zoom to In-N-Out and eat fresh, hot burgers and fries there until our heads explode."

Someday cheeseburgers? his stomach asked, sounding apologetic. *Fresh and hot In-N-Out Double-Doubles?*

"Someday," Rick said, wishing he believed it was true.

DO THE RIGHT THING

RICK HAD TRANSFERRED to a school within walking distance of home this year for fifth grade because his old math-and-science magnet school had changed his bus route last winter. While the old route had made him pretty sick, the new one had been agonizing. His parents had tried rearranging their schedule so one of them could drive him to school and home to the Herreras' to save him the embarrassment of losing his breakfast or lunch on the bus while horrified fellow students looked on. Adding exhausting hours to Mom's or Dad's already-epic driving days was hardly worth it—driving with his folks dialed back the motion sickness but didn't eliminate it.

Rick's town-house complex had a full block-long sidewalk with concrete right up to each front stoop, but once Rick crossed at the light to walk toward Eleanor Roosevelt Elementary, the sidewalks were broken and disconnected. The homeowners in the neighborhood between him and the school didn't seem to take much pride in keeping up their properties. Rick ended up walking to school across crumbling driveways and unkempt front yards, hoping not to get chased by too many dogs.

Walking this route the next morning, Rick noticed how the cars crawling along in the street didn't sound very oceanlike when you were next to them. Honking and hiccupping exhaust in his face, they made the hot August morning feel even hotter. He scanned the small empty lot where he'd found the ROAD WORK sign but didn't see anything else worth bringing home.

After dodging one tiny, yappy dog and entering Eleanor Roosevelt's double doors, he passed his ten-year-old neighbor, Mila Herrera, on his way to homeroom. She gave him a small smile while walking under the poster of Spike Lee telling them to DO THE RIGHT THING, but she didn't say anything.

Rick returned her smile. Her silence didn't bother him. He knew she wasn't a particularly talkative person. He'd been going to Mila's house after school every day since his brothers had moved out for college. He'd spent a good chunk of the past summer over there, too, since Aleks and Thomas had won scholarships to attend special summer civic engagement classes.

School had been in session for a week, and Mila was the only person he knew so far. He knew he could cope with being a loner; he just didn't want to be one. At his old magnet school, his classmates lived scattered around the city, and after a while his friends' parents had become unwilling to drive the distance to bring their kids to Rick's house. When several friends had started Pee Wee football, Rick had tried joining, too, so he could see them at practices and games, but having to lie prone on the bench trying to get his stomach to stop howling meant he wasn't much of a team player. He'd only made it to two practices before he gave up.

It was hard to start at a new school, but on the positive side, it meant shedding the nickname Carsick Rick. The odds were good he could protect himself from that nickname here. He also had a plan to fit in. He'd focus on joining conversations about the video game *Ninja Smash Warriors* (he'd reached the thirteenth level) and never mentioning his subscription to *Traffic Technology Today* to anyone. Not talking about his favorite hobby was definitely the way to go. When he was younger, he thought if he explained his Snarl Solutions well enough, other people would think they were as interesting as he did. But he'd learned his lesson in third grade when the teacher had taught them similes, describing comparisons using *like* or *as*, like "the vanilla milkshake was as white as snow." He'd read his long list out loud, including "traffic is like an ant farm," "traffic is like water drops chasing each other down a shower curtain," and "traffic is like pouring rice through a funnel." The similes didn't interest anyone. Even the teacher's eyes had glazed over. He wouldn't make that mistake here.

Rick struggled not to yawn through his English and

social studies classes, pretending to take notes but doodling instead. So far, his teachers were teaching stuff he'd already learned last year. He thought his parents weren't wrong to worry that Eleanor Roosevelt Elementary might be kind of a crummy school.

Art class promised to be different today, at least. The teacher tapped on the board with a pointer to get everyone's attention. She announced, "As promised, we have a special visitor today from the California Museum of Ancient Art to tell us about the Seven Wonders of the Ancient World. Professor, take it away."

The professor started up a slideshow. "Now, most of you probably know about the last standing Wonder of the World, the Great Pyramid of Giza in Egypt." He showed a picture of a yellow-hued pyramid surrounded by sand. "But there were others, including the Hanging Gardens of Babylon"—a painting of plants cascading over a white building with lots of pillars and stairs—"the Lighthouse of Alexandria"—another painting, of a super-tall lighthouse surrounded by clouds—"and the Colossus of Rhodes." This last one was a black-and-white sketch of a giant naked guy with a crown like the Statue of Liberty's.

The class immediately starting buzzing with laughter. "Settle down!" their teacher exclaimed. "This is very educational!" The professor looked flustered. Rick felt bad for him, so he raised his hand.

"Excuse me, who was the Colossus of Roads? Was he famous for building the first roads somewhere in the ancient world?" If that was true, Rick thought he'd enjoy learning more about him.

"No, no," the professor said, "not roads like we drive on, it's the Colossus of Rhodes, an island in the Greek archipelago. *RHodes.*" He made an emphatic breathy sound on the letter *h* and then clicked ahead in his slide-show to where Rick could see it written down. This slide had nothing but words and dates on it, so the students quieted down somewhat. "The Colossus was a bronze statue of the Greek sun god Helios, by far the tallest statue known to the public in two ninety-two BC." Rick pretended he was interested in the next details, because he could see the professor was getting his groove back, but was a little disappointed the discussion wasn't going to circle around to ancient freeways.

Rick doodled a fully clothed man standing over a freeway, holding a speed limit sign like a spear. He wrote *THE COLOSSUS OF ROADS* in angular Greek-looking let-ters underneath it. A much better nickname than Car-sick Rick, for sure. Was there a way to start up your own nickname? He looked around at his classmates. Nah, he'd stick with video games and hope for the best. He didn't need another nickname with a potential for provoking laughter.

At lunchtime, Rick found an empty seat at a cafeteria table with kids arguing over which video games were the best. He tried interjecting something about *Ninja Smash Warriors* into the conversation, but a kid sitting at the far end of the table widened his eyes and shook his head at Rick ever so slightly, so he clammed up.

After the final bell, he waited under the baking sun with the handful of students who walked home. The teachers wouldn't let the walkers leave until every school bus had been loaded and every car-line kid was picked up, presumably to protect vulnerable pedestrians from impatient parents speeding into and out of the school driveway. Almost no one walked at Eleanor Roosevelt Elementary, probably for the same reasons Mila caught the bus home instead of walking with Rick: disconnected sidewalks, few crosswalks, and territorial dogs.

When Rick got to the Herreras', Mrs. Herrera threw open the door at the first knock, hugging Rick and kissing him on the top of his head as she ushered him into the kitchen. She was an unstoppably huggy-kissy kind of lady. He didn't mind it so much as long as no one from school ever saw her doing it. Mila and her baby sister, Daniela, didn't count.

"Hungry, Rick? I can make you eggs, I can make you arepas, I have mangos." Mrs. Herrera tried to feed anyone who was sitting still, and made some really interesting food. Her arepas were these cornmeal pancake things she would grill on the stove and fill with stuff like shredded beef or chicken or butter and cheese.

"Thanks, Mrs. Herrera. If you have some arepas around, I would like one with that crumbly cheese," Rick said. "Hi, Mila. Hi, Baby Daniela." When he'd started coming last year, Mom had pulled Mrs. Herrera aside to explain that Rick would arrive sweaty and unable to say much after the ride and would have no interest in snacks for at least an hour. It was a nice change to walk right in and talk about food.

Mila sat at the table finishing some deep-yellow mango slices. "Hi," she said. She nearly always beat him home. (When she'd found out Rick was switching schools and would be walking, she'd asked his mom, "Doesn't Rick want to take the bus with me? The driver is really nice, and our street is the first stop in the afternoon." When his mom had started to answer, "Oh, the bus doesn't work for Rick," he'd clutched her hand to stop her from revealing anything humiliating. He wanted as few people as possible knowing the details of his affliction.)

Seven-month-old Baby Daniela was nodding and blinking slowly, buckled securely into a plastic chair clipped onto the edge of the kitchen table, a shred of mango clutched in one fist. As Rick sat down, he watched her eyes close and her head sink to her chest. She didn't relinquish her grip on the mango, though. Not even a nap could get between Baby Daniela and a munchie.

Mrs. Herrera put a plate in front of him with two buttery, toasty arepas topped with a crumbly fresh cheese from the Mexican grocery store, plus a cut-up orange and a glass of guava punch. *Hooray!* his stomach burbled. No matter what you asked for, Mrs. Herrera served you at least one thing more. Her snacks made her one of his stomach's favorite people. If it wouldn't have embarrassed his parents, Rick would have suggested they regularly invite themselves over here for dinner.

"Lots of homework today, kids? Or do you want to join me and Abuelita and watch the race?" Mrs. Herrera asked. When the family wasn't watching soccer games broadcast from other countries, they were watching international bike races. Both Dr. and Mrs. Herrera had special cycling outfits in the same colors as the Venezuelan flag, and Dr. Herrera rode his bike to work as a medical resident over ten miles each way. The only person in their house who owned a car was Mrs. Herrera's mother, an ancient lady they all called Abuelita.

"I've got some graphing I really want to tackle," said Rick.

"And I've got word problems I didn't finish in class," said Mila.

"Well, try your best to keep it down in here," Mrs. Herrera said, winking. She often kidded them about their noisiness, because Mila and Rick could sit together scarcely speaking for hours, doing homework, playing Uno, or watching Cartoon Network. Mila was into art and was always sketching stuff like castles and dragons and unicorns, while Rick worked on his Snarl Solutions. "When you finish, come join us to watch the mountain stage of the race." She waved her hand in front of her face as if cooling off a sudden fever. "Those racers ride like angels. But such skinny angels!" Then she noticed Baby Daniela's head tipping even farther down her chest. The girl let out a little baby snore. "Daniela, *mi vida*, let's get you in the crib," Mrs. Herrera said, unbuckling her and tugging the mango shred out of her hand. (*Mi vida*, which means "my life" in Spanish, was what the Herreras called each other.) She grunted as she lifted Daniela and laid the baby's head on her shoulder, murmuring in her ear. "If you grow up to be a bicycle racer, you will be a strong, sturdy sprinter, not a skinny mountain climber."

Mila opened her backpack and pulled out her homework. "Is your graphing for school, or are you working on another one of your street things?"

"One of my street things," Rick said, pulling out two rulers, his best mechanical pencil, and his graph-paper pad. He and his dad had mapped out the best routes to the two events Smotch had catered yesterday, but last night, after the pizza had finally come and been consumed, he'd spent some time on Google Street View virtually visiting these routes. He'd examined the road signs along both the surface streets and the 5 Freeway, and his fingers were itching to sketch out Snarl Solutions based on what he'd seen. Once he studied a map, digitally or on paper, he had it memorized for good.

Mila said, "Oh, okay," and started in on her sheet of word problems. Rick took a bite of his arepa and sucked the juice from a slice of orange. They both scratched away with their pencils in easy silence.

The kitchen around Rick faded. He didn't hear Mrs. Herrera cheering cyclists' names as they cruised up hills.

He didn't hear Abuelita saying, "If I could have raced bicycles when I was younger, I would have gone so fast, they would have nicknamed me Meteoro," and Mrs. Herrera answering, "Really? You'd have ridden like a meteor? Then why do you drive so slowly now?" He was lost in a happy place of straight lines and road signs, his stomach chirping delighted comments about the arepas.

Rick reached for the last piece of orange and knocked his pencil to the floor. When he picked it up, he saw that Mila had put away her homework and was watching him.

"Did you know you've been humming?" she asked.

"Humming? I don't think so," Rick said.

"You've had the biggest smile on your face, and you've been humming at your graph paper," Mila said. "You've done it before, but never this loudly. You must really like what you're doing."

Rick looked back at the solutions he'd finalized. With the changes he'd made, he could see his parents having a smooth, flowing trip along the routes they'd taken yesterday instead of being late. He hummed the first notes of the *Ninja Smash Warriors* theme song. He heard himself this time.

Mila covered her smile with her hand.

"Okay, okay, I do hum. I hum awesome ninja-inspiring tunes," Rick acknowledged. "And I do like what I'm doing. See these, here, here, here, here, here, *annnd* here? If someone could switch these signs, move these other ones slightly, and decrease the speed limit near this freeway exit like so, enough drivers would drive properly. That'd tip the balance and things would smooth out for everyone. Small changes tend to cause a chain reaction, like in an ant farm. Once a few ants figure out how to cooperate, the rest of them start doing it too. Ants don't have traffic jams."

Mila responded with a polite but unenthusiastic, "Oh, okay." His shoulders slumped a tiny bit. He questioned for the gazillionth time why the patterns he saw were invisible to everyone he knew. He wondered if a well-trained hunter or tracker who could point out a tiny detail and say "A single male raccoon walked south by this tree two days ago carrying a crawfish in its mouth" had friends and family looking over their shoulders saying, "What? You mean that smudge on the ground means something?"

Mila scrunched up her face a little, like she was trying to think of something more to say. "Maybe you should send these to the people who put up the signs."

Rick shook his head. "I've tried that loads of times, but no one has ever emailed me back. Maybe they can tell my emails are written by a kid, so they think they're not important." In fact, the email address he'd found was supposed to be for traffic complaints, so he'd started wondering if every complaint email fell automatically into some electronic Department of Transportation recycle bin. He sighed. His Snarl Solutions seemed destined to remain nothing more than pieces of graph paper until he was old enough to get a job making them real.

They're still good, his stomach said. *Feels nice to imagine a better world.*

Mila stood up and pushed in her chair. "Want to come watch the race?" she said just as the doorbell rang. Mrs. Herrera dashed in from the living room to open it to Rick's mom. Mrs. Herrera gave her a quick hug and kiss and said, "Nice to see you early today! Come join us!" She then dashed back to the television, where Abuelita was loudly encouraging a cyclist to pick up his pace.

"Can't today, Maridol. Thanks anyway," Mom called into the living room. "Hi, Mila. Ready, Rick?" Her curly black hair was back in a messy ponytail, and she had a smear of what looked like mustard on one of her round cheeks.

"I guess," Rick said, gathering up his stuff. "Why are you early, Mom?"

"Bye, everyone!" Mom called out as they left, then answered him, "Why am I early? Just lucky, getting to spend some extra time with you, Roo."

Rick made a face. Another nickname it was time to shed. He was working on reducing his folks' fondness for calling him Roo, after Kanga's baby boy in *Winnie-the-Pooh*. In spite of asking him to demonstrate more Pre-Teen Responsibility, they often seemed stuck seeing him as a baby that needed to be protected in a pouch. "Rick, Mom, it's Rick," he corrected her.

"Right, that's what I said, Rick-who-is-definitely-not-a-Roo," she answered with a smile. But her smile looked strained.

NOT JUST FOR DUCTS

MOM UNLOCKED THEIR door and made a pit stop at the bathroom. Dad was already home, sitting at the kitchen table with a calculator and a binder full of papers. He stood up and started clearing things to the couch. "Hey, kiddo. Wash up and help set the table. A happy cabbage-roll-free dinner awaits us all. Mom and I went shopping, and we're going to make spaghetti and meatballs."

Double hooray! said Rick's stomach. *Life is good.* But Rick noticed Dad's smile also wasn't up to its usual level either. He looked as worn out as he had the night before.

"Dad, what's up? Why are you both home so early? Didn't you have one of your dinner deliveries scheduled for today?" Mom and Dad sometimes served their food buffet-style but more often dropped it off. They regularly served two, sometimes three lunches a day and did a couple of dinner drop-offs per week. Since Rick's brothers had moved out, they'd stopped doing weekend events or anything that could run late into the evening.

"Why didn't anyone tell me I had mustard on my

cheek?" he heard Mom calling from behind the bathroom door, then running water.

"The dinner delivery canceled their contract earlier this week," Dad said. Some places had standing contracts for food to be delivered on certain dates and times. "But since that means spaghetti and meatballs, it's not the worst news."

Mom came back in and shushed Dad. "Let's not talk contracts. Let's enjoy a nice meal as a family." She set a pot of water on the stove, sprinkled salt into it, and began chopping garlic and tomatoes.

Rick washed his hands in the kitchen sink. It was a small kitchen, so he had to lean around his mom to get down three plates. He noticed something. "Mom, you might want to know, you have mustard on your ear."

"Must have missed that spot," she said. "I suppose it's my badge of successful-cooking honor. We got rave reviews at a lunch buffet we served today. Can you get it off? My hands are all tomatoey."

Rick ripped off a piece of paper towel and swiped the brownish-yellow blob off Mom's earlobe.

"What a good son," she said. "Now please get the meat out of the fridge."

Rick handed her the package of ground beef and got the table set. When the meal was ready, they sat down and started passing bowls. Rick told them about the school visit from the ancient art professor, leaving out the naked statue part. Not an appropriate dinnertime image.

When there was a pause in the conversation, Mom cleared her throat and said, "Sooooo. Dad says you did well with yesterday's trial of Pre-Teen Responsibility. We were wondering if you might like to do a little more of that? Maybe spend afternoons over here alone instead of at the Herreras'?"

His stomach made a noise of protest. "I really like it at the Herreras', Mom. I'd rather stay there. Being home by myself would be boring."

Mom and Dad exchanged a long look. She jutted her chin at Dad as if prompting him. He said, "Your mom and I have been talking, and we don't want you to miss opportunities to, er, explore and develop new skills."

Watch out, his stomach warned. *Are they going to start driving us to activities again? Did we learn nothing from football practice?*

"Whoops, forgot to put out the salad." Mom stood up and returned to the table with the salad bowl. She also handed Rick a spiral-bound book labeled *Webelos Cub Scout Handbook*. "What do you think about this? We called the local Cub Scout master and asked if there was a way for you to participate without having to drive to anything. He said if we sign off on your work and get it to him, he'd be happy to include you. He said you'd be welcome to attend meetings once a week virtually through Skype or FaceTime."

Rick looked at the cover of the handbook. It had a picture of uniformed boys setting up a tent in a forest.

"What would I do, set up a tent in the living room on camera like I'm in quarantine?"

"Not like you're in quarantine, like you're a smart kid who knows his limits!" Mom said indignantly, giving him another meatball. "You'd work on completing tasks at home to earn activity pins. Look, we know extra driving isn't an option for this family, so we have to be creative. We're trying to think of ways to use technology to help you connect with some new people and develop new skills."

Where is this coming from? Rick wondered. "Sorry, Mom, I don't understand why you came up with this idea. I'd say changing schools is enough change for now."

"Things might be fine if we don't do this," Dad said to Mom. They exchanged a long, odd glance, battling about something via their eyeballs.

Mom appeared to win, because she spoke next. "It's something your father and I have talked about, and we'd really like you to give it a try.

Rick grudgingly flipped through the Webelos handbook. "Anything in here about traffic patterns?"

"Oh, hon, there's so much good stuff," said Mom. "For instance, in October, there's a Duct Tape Regatta, where participants build a boat capable of floating while holding a piece of fruit. Try something new. You never know where your true talents might lie."

Aha, that was it. This had something to do with his mom's concern that he spent too much time and energy on his Snarl Solutions. Rick wished he had a good way to defend what he was pretty sure was his one true talent. Mom took the handbook from him and flipped to a page that read *Not Just for Ducts*.

"You can't tell me this doesn't sound fun!" She read aloud, "'With enough duct tape on hand, a Scout can do practically anything: use it in first aid, emergency rescue, as a building tool, or to design an entertaining game,'" and added, "See, there are lots of projects you could work on after school, keeping your hands and mind busy."

Dad said, "I could pick up a boat's worth of duct tape from the hardware store."

Rick sighed. "I guess I could think about it."

"That's all we ask, kiddo," Mom said, passing him back the Scout handbook. "Read this later! I bet it will get you excited."

Rick set the handbook next to his plate. He twirled a big knot of pasta onto his fork. If more change was in the cards, he needed more good things to be added to his life, not have already-good things like the Herreras' replaced. He'd come up with a nice way to say no to his mom's ideas.

Hours later, Rick was supposed to be asleep. But the ROAD WORK sign, leaning up against the wall next to his computer, caught the light from the streetlamp outside and gleamed at him. It was so cool to have a real sign he could touch.

He climbed quietly out of bed to start up his computer.

He opened his email to send the two traffic Snarl Solutions he'd come up with this afternoon to the Los Angeles Department of Transportation. Maybe some new person would start reading the emails this week and get blown away by his ideas.

To keep him company on his computer screen while he typed, Rick opened a digital map of the 210 Freeway, which ran behind his house. At this time of night, it was green. Most traffic-alert websites highlighted places without problems in green and places with problems in red. The green areas struck Rick as radiating an almost liquid peace, like pictures he'd seen of seaweed fronds billowing with the tide, while the glaring scarlet patches where cars were jammed up pulsed with misery, like bleeding scabs picked from a skateboarder's knees.

Ew, red like scabs? How about red like dried ketchup? his stomach said. *And instead of green like seaweed, green like something tasty. Like mint ice cream, or lime lollipops, or guacamole.* Rick let his stomach continue mulling over tasty green things.

"Let's just tell the boy," he heard Dad say from his parents' bedroom. Mom shushed him. Of course, Rick's ears pricked up. He stopped typing and leaned his chair toward the wall between their bedrooms.

"I think he's old enough to understand our family finances," Dad said in a slightly lower voice. "Learning to manage money is part of growing up."

"No. Parents take care of their children, not the other

way around," Mom said in a decisive tone. "Besides, I don't want Rick to feel responsible for us losing money."

Rick frowned. How was he responsible for something like that?

She went on. "Of our three sons, we certainly can't expect Rick to help."

"That's true," Dad agreed.

Rick listened even harder. *What can't I be expected to help with?*

Mom went on. "He doesn't know how many contracts we lost last year taking the time to drive him to school and the Herreras', or how much canceling weekend jobs has cost us. And I don't want him to. Our poor little car-sick Roo, life is hard enough for him."

Rick resisted the urge to call out, *It's Rick, Mom, not Roo!*

Dad said, "So we don't tell him about that. We tell him the other half of the truth, that traffic has become so atrocious, we never know if we'll be able to deliver food on time that our clients won't find too cold, too dried out, tasting too much like exhaust fumes. We're losing business because of it and need to cut back on expenses. Explaining that will make more sense to him than 'you're old enough to be by yourself after school.' You saw his face at dinner. He thinks we're nuts to suggest he stay home alone to work on Cub Scout projects."

"I don't want him to worry, and I don't want him to become one of those kids who does nothing but play video games alone after school. I don't know what else to do." Mom's voice got even quieter as she moved toward the other side of the room. Rick strained to hear. She was saying something about how they wouldn't be able to pay the Herreras for after-school care after the middle of next month. "I haven't told Maridol yet," he heard clearly as Mom opened the bedroom door and headed for the bathroom. "You know she'd insist on doing it for free, and that's not right."

Dad called after her, "Pretty soon, that's going to be the least of our worries."

"Shhh!" Mom replied.

Rick ran his fingers through his hair. What did Dad mean that not being able to pay the Herreras anymore would soon be the least of their worries? What else wouldn't they be able to pay for? That sounded like more already-good things might get replaced. And he really didn't like hearing that they didn't expect him to be of any help. He wasn't some hopeless preteen kangaroo they still had to lug around in a pouch.

You are not hopeless, his stomach said staunchly. *You are very hopeful. Hopeful and helpful. In fact, you could be the helpingest helper who ever helped. Who else in this family has figured out how to fix traffic? Your Snarl Solutions could make everything smooth for Smotch.*

"Yeah, but..." Rick sighed. He scanned the maps on his walls, and the Snarl Solutions taped below them. He knew each one by heart. They did seem like good, solid ideas, with the potential to smooth out so much. "Who's going to listen to me?" His eyes flicked back to the draft of his email. What could he write that would make a difference? That would get someone with the authority and the heavy-duty tools necessary to give his ideas a try?

Green M&M's! gurgled his stomach. *That's another tasty green thing! Sorry, I'll focus now. How do we get your ideas set up on the streets?*

Rick thought and thought, then typed and typed.

→ → →

When he got to school the next day, Rick was in a grouchy mood. He'd sent last night's email, which used every synonym for the word *please* he could find, but had no faith anyone at the Los Angeles Department of Transportation would pay it any attention. He needed a better idea. Maybe if he showed up in person and insisted at the top of his voice that he had valuable information that could save the city from itself? But the Department of Transportation was four freeway interchanges away. How did you get a powerful adult's attention when you were eleven and couldn't go anywhere?

When he walked into the cafeteria, he heard a "Psst!" from the tray-return area. The kid who'd given him the head shake at lunch yesterday was motioning him over.

"You're new, right?" the kid asked.

"Right," Rick said. "Transferred here this year. My name's Rick." He stuck out his hand.

The kid waved off the handshake. "You might not want

to be seen getting friendly with me. You could end up with a dumb nickname as fallout. I moved here last year and I'm still trying to shed the nicknames I got saddled with."

Rick said, "I know exactly how much that stinks."

The kid nodded. "If I had it to do over again, I wouldn't've talked at lunch until I felt sure someone already liked the thing I wanted to talk about. Most of the names I've been called aren't even imaginative, just mean. I'm grateful that one of them isn't too bad. I can take it when they call me Tennis." He twisted his lips in a not-so-grateful way. "But it's the way they say it. Like I'm not from the same planet as they are. If you follow sports other than basketball, and any team other than the LA Lakers, this is not the school to mention it in. Basically, don't talk about anything that might be seen as 'out of the norm.'" He made air quotes around the last four words. "When I heard you say something about *Ninja Smash Warriors*, I knew I had to give you a heads-up. *Ninja Smash Warriors* is out. The new game is *Beat Down*." The kid glanced around. "Okay, hope that helps you out, Rick. I know I wish someone had given me the scoop when I'd started here. Gotta go."

"Wait, what's your real name?" Rick asked. But Tennis had slipped through the crowd and was gone. Rats. There was no way Mom would let Rick play the violent online multiplayer *Beat Down*, and their internet connection wasn't fast enough anyway. He knew some basic stuff about the Lakers basketball team, but it sounded like he was going to have to watch their games religiously if he wanted to fit in.

On the way home, the yappy dog launched a surprise attack from a whole different yard. Or it might have been a different dog. Either way, Rick sprinted out of its territory. He was sweating when Mila opened the door for him. He dropped his backpack on the kitchen table and slumped in a chair. Mila sat down and started doodling unicorns on her math notebook.

"Mom's giving Baby Daniela a bath," Mila said. "She said to tell you to help yourself to Abuelita's pound cake."

"Whatever," he said in a dull voice. Mila raised her eyebrows at him but said nothing.

He unzipped his backpack and pulled out some graph paper. The Webelos handbook spilled out too, open to the page celebrating the miraculous powers of duct tape.

Mila pointed to the page. "Hey," she said. She disappeared into her room, then came out carrying a pink-and-green wallet. She handed it to Rick.

"Thanks?" he said, continuing his grouch, turning it over in his hands. It was woven from alternative colors out of some thick shiny stuff.

"You know how I started Girl Scouts last week? Our troop leader is teaching us ways to turn ordinary materials into art. It's made out of duct tape."

"There's pink and green duct tape?" Rick asked, slightly ungrouchified. He really shouldn't waste what might be his final weeks at the Herreras' in a bad mood.

"We had green, pink, blue, red, silver glitter, and purple. I wanted to try weaving a multi-color bag, but I didn't have time at the meeting since Abuelita dropped me off late. She drove so slowly, there was a mom with a stroller on the sidewalk who was going the same speed as we were. Abuelita kept waving to her. I probably could have gotten there faster on my scooter."

Rick shook his head, picturing Abuelita sailing her giant boat of a car down the street with her window down, chatting with the stroller-striding mom as she held up traffic for blocks behind her. Maybe there were some things his traffic solutions couldn't fix. Thank goodness there was only one Abuelita.

He opened the wallet. There was a one-dollar bill inside, and a handmade ID card with a unicorn on it that said *Mila Herrera, Artist*.

Mrs. Herrera and Abuelita walked into the room together, cheerfully arguing in Spanish. "*Hola*, Rick," Mrs. Herrera said. "Abuelita, you had better leave in a couple of minutes so you can get Mila to her Scout meeting on time. You know how you drive."

Abuelita tucked an errant strand of gray hair back into her bun and made a *Phsst!* noise. "Trust me, I'm the best driver in Los Angeles. I'll deliver her safe and on time."

Mila rolled her eyes at Rick and mouthed the words *so slow*.

Abuelita untied her red chili pepper-patterned apron, slipped it over her head, and hung it on a hook near the stove. "Ricardo," she said to Rick, "the cake I made will give you energy to run around and have fun. Not that you can run around in this neighborhood. Too many cars are going too fast. If only everyone would drive nice and slow, take their time, this city would be safer for all the children. Kids playing outside, that's more important than going fast." She glanced at the clock on the wall. "Oopsy-doodle. Mila, we'd better get going."

"Okay," said Mila, getting up and pushing in her chair. She said to Rick, "I forgot to tell you, my Girl Scout meeting is at an artist's house today. You know that house near Yum Num Donuts with the metal sculptures in front?"

Rick said, "I haven't been to Yum Num Donuts before."

"Oh. If you try it sometime, look for the house with giant metal chickens and flags down the street," she said, shrugging into her shamrock-green Junior Girl Scout vest. "See you later."

"See you later," Rick echoed.

Mrs. Herrera put a thick slice of pound cake down in front of him. "You look like you're a million miles away, in a place you don't want to be. They working you too hard at school?"

"Thanks, Mrs. Herrera. No, school's okay. It's other stuff I can't figure out. Stuff that might as well be a million miles away."

"You'll get there," she answered, patting his back. "Kids aren't supposed to figure everything out. You're supposed to try things, mess up, then try other things. And you're supposed to eat good cake! And maybe a smoothie, too? Let me see what I can whip up for you."

I love it here, his stomach sighed. *Please figure out a way we still get to come.*

THE BEST DRIVER IN LA

MILA RETURNED RIGHT before Mom and Dad were scheduled to come get Rick. She held something behind her back. "Guess what I get to do?" she said, smiling.

The pound cake and strawberry-banana smoothie had gone a long way to getting Rick out of his grouchy slump. He raised his hand. "Ooh! Ooh! I know this one! You get to...drive so slowly with Abuelita that you actually go backward in time!"

Mila quietly cracked up and looked around to make sure Abuelita hadn't heard him. "We were late again, but it was okay, because we got to do such amazing stuff. Look!" What she pulled from around her back was the last thing Rick would have guessed: a SPEED LIMIT 35 road sign. But the 5 had been painted with green and purple paint to look like a curvy fire-breathing dragon. Mila put it on the kitchen table so they could both admire it.

"What is this?" Rick asked, baffled and intrigued. He touched the dragon's tail.

"It's our new service project! The artist's house we went to, Anna Diamond, she creates public art that's displayed all around Los Angeles. My troop leader talked to her and she talked to her sister, who works for the city, and asked if we could make a public art project out of any recyclable materials the city wasn't using. Now we get to paint old road signs with special reflective paint!" Mila didn't usually talk this much or this loudly. Rick could tell how thrilled she was.

"They gave you each an old road sign to paint?" Rick asked.

"More than one—bunches. When we're done with them, Ms. Diamond said she knows different neighborhoods that want them hung up in parks, on old buildings, decorating medians or ugly fences, stuff like that. Ms. Diamond said we can really make a difference in people's lives when they see our art. It'll remind them how beautiful any ordinary thing can be. She said Picasso said, 'Art washes away from the soul the dust of everyday life.'"

"The signs are pretty perfect the way they are, though," Rick said. His fingers itched to grab the sign, take it home with him, and wash the paint off in the bathtub.

"Oh, I thought you'd like it," Mila said, less excited-sounding. "I've seen you sketch road signs like this on your graph paper. I got permission to bring it home and show it to you and my family."

"Sorry," Rick apologized. "This is definitely...creative."

Mollified, Mila continued, "I'm going to finish this one at Ms. Diamond's house next week. Our troop leader said instead of our regular meetings, we're going to focus on this for a whole month."

Rick blinked, momentarily overcome, thinking of the multitude of perfectly useful signs about to be covered in Girl Scout paint.

Mila traced her finger over the 3 next to her dragon. "I'm going to make the three into a knight battling the dragon, and see if I can make each letter of *Speed Limit* into a different mythical creature. Ms. Diamond has a California condor made out of bent street signs flying over her front door, and her backyard is a sculpture garden with twisty paths so you can get lost among her creations. And there are sculptures in her house, too. When you walk in her front door, you're in this big room without much furniture. Lots of space to spread out. Some of those huge freeway signs are going to be delivered next week."

"Wow," Rick said. "How is she getting them to her house?"

"I told you, her sister works for the city. I think she's the manager of traffic, or transport. She gets the signs to Ms. Diamond."

"Wait, do you mean her sister runs the Department of Transportation?" Rick asked.

Mila pressed her lips together. "Maybe. That sounds right."

"And she's coming to drop off more signs to the Girl Scouts? Next week?" Rick involuntarily clapped his hands together. A very important city official, someone with authority over road signs, would be visiting his side of

Los Angeles. Maybe he could talk to her about his Snarl Solutions.

"Yup. We're supposed to make her a thank-you note to bring with us. Ms. Diamond says her sister is very particular about thank-you notes. Why?"

The doorbell rang and Mrs. Herrera called out, "Rick! Your dad is here for you!"

"Mila," Rick blurted. "Is there any way I can join your Girl Scout troop?"

→ → →

That evening Rick found out, much to his relief, that he needn't become a Girl Scout to attend the next meeting. Mila had asked her mom, Mrs. Herrera had made some calls, and the troop leader and Ms. Diamond had said family and friends were welcome to participate in the painting project.

Rick had then gotten his parents' permission to go. "We're happy you're trying something new, but...painting with the Girl Scouts? With Abuelita driving you?" Mom had asked, feeling his forehead. "I don't know about this."

Rick's stomach was giving him furious this-isn't-worth-it signals, but he ignored it. "Mom, this is important to me. I think I can handle it. I'll bring lots of double-reinforced bags for the ride to and from Anna Diamond's house."

As soon as he mentioned Anna Diamond's name, his dad got excited.

"Anna Diamond's a street art legend! I've always suspected she was behind painting those giant cat faces on the Los Angeles River drains. Sweetheart, if the boy is willing to try to get there to learn from her, we have to say yes. It's an amazing opportunity," he said.

"Who am I to stand in the way of an amazing opportunity?" Mom said with a bewildered shrug. "I guess Rick's going."

Next, Rick searched the LA Department of Transportation website and found a picture of its general manager, Mrs. Althea Torres. She was the only woman listed, so he thought she was probably the artist's sister. He studied her face to see whether she'd be one of those people who dismiss what kids have to say simply because they're kids. It was impossible to tell. She looked elegant and serious. Well, he'd wear his most grown-up pants and T-shirt.

Finally, Rick found the address of Yum Num Donuts on its website and looked at its location on a map. His stomach did a somersault. It was six miles away on Balboa Boulevard, a street with multiple freeway entrances where traffic often tangled in stop-and-go knots.

So, going there was a good idea in theory. Too bad we'll be staying home instead, his stomach said.

"No, we're going. We have to," he told his stomach. "It's my only chance to talk to Mrs. Torres."

Maybe you could ride your bike there? his stomach pleaded. Rick owned a bike, but with so many broken sidewalks in his neighborhood, he didn't ride much. And riding on the road was too scary. Once, when he was ped-aling on the street with his parents, someone's rearview mirror had brushed his elbow. He'd glanced in the window of the car and seen a guy steering with his knees, a cup of coffee in one hand, his phone in the other. His parents would occasionally ride with him down to the local cycling path for a family outing, but they hadn't done that in a while. He was pretty sure his mom had seen the coffee-and-phone guy too.

Rick asked his stomach to buck up. "What matters is that we get there, and that we convince Mrs. Torres to listen to me. Stomach, keep your eyes on the prize. We've got to convince her to start trying my Snarl Solutions in the places Smotch needs them. This is how we can help Mom and Dad."

I will be brave, his stomach said. But Rick could still feel it wobbling.

→ → →

The following Tuesday afternoon, Rick followed Mila and Abuelita to their carport. Mila carried her partially painted speed limit sign and a homemade thank-you card. Rick had his school backpack slung over his shoulder, a manila folder with his best Snarl Solutions tucked inside, along with double-reinforced bags. He was wearing his khaki pants, a plain black T-shirt, and his black In-N-Out Burger cap. He thought it made him look sort of professional. A little taller, at least.

I can do this, he repeated to himself. *I can do this. No matter how Abuelita drives, I can do this.*

Abuelita's 1952 Cadillac Eldorado was fire-engine red with tailfins. It sat in the carport like a long, fat tropical fish. Rick climbed into the backseat.

We can do this? his stomach asked.

We can, he told it as confidently as possible.

One mile out of the driveway, he knew he couldn't. He was going to die. Abuelita was not only slow, she was swerving hypnotically back and forth across the road, angry cars behind her laying on their horns. Rick grabbed a handful of carsickness bags out of his backpack and clutched them tightly. His stomach bellowed the unhappy moose noise.

Abuelita glanced at him in the rearview mirror. "Are you all right?"

Mila answered for him. "He's turning a funny color. I don't think he feels well."

Abuelita pulled into a 7-Eleven and turned off the car. She turned around and got a good look at Rick. Her eyes widened in alarm. "Ricardo! What do you need?"

He needed someone to peel him off the seat and lay him down in a small hole where he would never be asked to move or speak again. But he had to find a way to survive the next five miles. He had to meet the head of the Department of Transportation and impress her with his awesomeness. "I'm...fine...," he croaked.

"Did he say he was dying? *Pobrecito*, poor boy!"

Mila said, "We should probably turn around and take him home."

"Not...home...please...can...make it." He tried to push his face into a smile.

The wrinkles on Abuelita's forehead deepened. "Do you feel this way from the motion of the car?" she asked.

Rick managed a nod.

Her forehead smoothed. "I know what to do. Rest now. Breathe. And tell me when you are ready for us to move again." Abuelita reached into the glove compartment and pulled out a pair of red leather driving gloves. Each had a small brass button at the wrist. She slipped them onto her hands and snapped the buttons closed with relish.

Mila leaned over Rick and wound his window down for him. He breathed in the afternoon air and stared at the angles of the 7 in the 7-Eleven sign, willing his stomach to give him a break. When he felt he was back from the brink, he let out a sigh. "Better now."

Abuelita gave him a firm nod. "I will take care of you, Ricardo. Trust me. I am the best driver in LA."

Rick tried to prepare himself for the next onslaught of nausea. He was hit by a wave of surprise instead.

Abuelita pulled back out onto the street. Instead of slowing down cars behind her for blocks, she smoothly began passing every car ahead of her like they were standing still. She didn't have to tap her brakes even once, soaring under every green stoplight. Rick managed a glance at the speedometer, but she wasn't breaking any speed limits. Abuelita was somehow obeying all the traffic laws in the smoothest possible way.

When they glided to a stop at the curb in front of Anna Diamond's one-story adobe house, Rick's stomach had nothing to say. He thought it might be in shock.

Abuelita removed her driving gloves. "That was okay for you, Ricardo? Not feeling so sick now?" she asked.

Rick nodded. If everyone drove like that, there'd be no need for Snarl Solutions or discussions with his stomach.

"I'll be back for you kids in a couple of hours," Abuelita said. "Have fun!"

They got out, Rick with his backpack, Mila carrying her dragon-decorated sign. They wordlessly watched Abuelita pull away, the big car once again slowly weaving like a placid red fish undulating upriver.

Ms. Diamond's yard had no grass, only sandy soil, desert plants, and sculptures. He and Mila silently navigated the flagstone walkway to the front door. "She always tells Mami and Papi she's the best driver in LA," Mila finally said.

"Maybe she is, sometimes," Rick said. He tried to simply be grateful for the fact he felt like a normal human being and not think about which of Abuelita's driving styles he'd get on the way home.

Mila rang the doorbell. Rick eyed the California condor above the door, made from contorted green street signs that had once labeled Valley Road, Tyler Street, and Memory Lane. He looked over his shoulder and saw the Yum Num Donuts sign illuminated down the street:

COME ON IN FOR FRESH DON TS. THE ONLY THING MISS-ING IS "U."

A woman with spiky black hair answered the door, wearing a wild parrot-print blouse that billowed around her ample frame. "Welcome, chickadees," she said. Standing guard inside the door, a sculpture of a rooster made from a rusted frying pan stood tall on stiltlike legs. The rooster held a bouquet of real lollipops in his beak.

Rick introduced himself. "I'm Mila's neighbor Rick Rusek. Thanks for letting me come."

"Call me Ms. Diamond. Always happy to encourage young artists. Come in, come in." She beckoned them past the rooster with her paint-spattered hands. "Paintbrushes and paints are over there. Grab any sign you like, find an open spot, and set your imaginations free! Whatever you make, I guarantee it will lift your fellow Angelenos' hearts when they see it."

The front of the house was open and airy, like it had been hollowed out into one large space for elaborate art-making. The cream-colored, rough-textured walls were hung with framed abstract paintings and odd objects, like animal antlers with holes drilled into them and a guitar shaped like a banana. The brick-red tile floor had been strewn with several drop cloths, but based on the array of stains Rick could see peeking from between them, Ms. Diamond wasn't bothered by spilled paint.

About a dozen Girl Scouts were eagerly sorting through

a sizable stack of road signs against the back wall. A couple of Scouts were already kneeling on drop cloths, busily painting their chosen signs. Two women were dolloping various colors onto plastic palettes. "That's my troop leader and her assistant," Mila told Rick. She introduced him to them, and one of them said, "Let us know if either of you need help getting started. And there's a padded mailing envelope over there for the thank-you cards."

"I think we're good," Mila said. She laid her dragon sign down on a drop cloth and said to Rick, "As soon as I put my card in the envelope, I'm going to get started. Why don't you go choose a sign and you can set up here next to me?"

"Sure," Rick said absently. He watched one girl using broad, splashy strokes to turn an entire ONE WAY sign purple. Rick wanted to explain to her what a waste of a perfectly good ONE WAY sign it was. He looked away and said under his breath, "Focus. Act professional. Remember why you're here."

Ms. Diamond finished ushering in another girl and headed for an untidy desk in the corner. Rick followed her. "Hi, er, Ms. Diamond. Mila said some big freeway signs were getting delivered today. Did they get here yet?" he asked.

"Not yet, but they should be here shortly. We'll continue concentrating on the smaller individual signs today and save the big signs for group work next time. Please, please, get started. Don't be shy." She sat in her rolling desk chair and it let out a squeak. "I want you young creators to feel empowered to make art everywhere you go, and find art everywhere you look."

"Yup, thanks," Rick said, not really listening. He'd assumed he'd need a long chunk of time to get himself back to normal after driving with Abuelita, so this extra time was an unexpected gift. He put down his backpack and unzipped it. He took out the manila folder on which he'd printed the words *Traffic Solutions* in his best-ever handwriting.

He closed his eyes and practiced his opening line for when Mrs. Torres arrived. *I'm Rick Rusek, and I think I can solve problems for both of us.* Then he'd confidently hand the folder to her. He'd read that if you handed a thing to people confidently before they really knew what it was, they'd take it automatically. Once Mrs. Torres opened the folder, once she looked at his Snarl Solutions, he was hoping they'd do the rest of his talking for him. "Yes, I see," Mrs. Torres would say. "These are precisely what our city needs. I will implement them immediately, and do the same with any other ideas you send me."

The sound of a large vehicle pulling into the driveway outside made his eyes pop open. "There they are now," Ms. Diamond said, standing and making the chair squeak again.

IF YOU CAN DREAM IT, YOU CAN DO IT

RICK WAITED FOR Mrs. Torres to come in, his lips getting ready to form *I'm Rick Rusek*. Instead, a tall guy with ropy muscles entered from the side door. "Where do you want this load?"

"Right up against this wall, please. I'll get the furniture dolly from the shed," Ms. Diamond said, disappearing out the same door.

"You're not Mrs. Torres," Rick said.

"Nope," the guy said. "And I wouldn't want to be."

"Are you a traffic engineer?" Rick asked.

"Nope again. And I wouldn't want to be that, either. I like being a delivery guy for the city."

Rick was at a loss. His mouth really wanted to start saying *I'm Rick Rusek, and I think I can solve problems* to someone, but this was not the right someone. Mila must have misunderstood.

Ms. Diamond returned with a couple of speed limit signs under her arm and said to the delivery guy, "I put the dolly next to the tailgate. That's one full truck. I'll help unload, but would you first like to see some of the art you're helping us create?" She motioned him closer to the drop cloths. The delivery guy shrugged and followed her. Rick followed both of them. He didn't know what else to do.

The two nearest Scouts were absorbed in their work. One was painting a jungle populated by sapphire tigers. The other had the purple-plastered ONE WAY sign. She appeared to be transforming it into a stout purple alligator. "Heh," the delivery guy said, cracking a smile. "You're going to let blue tigers and purple alligators loose on the streets of LA? Well, let's not dilly-dally. This looks important."

Rick stood clutching his manila folder to his chest and watched the delivery guy and Ms. Diamond bring in dozens of signs of all sizes and colors. The pile they made was beyond awesome. There were speed limit signs in every multiple of 5 from 15 to 70. There were signs there to fix nearly every traffic puzzle Rick had ever dreamed up. When the green freeway signs came in on the dolly, they were so much bigger than he'd realized. His brain felt a bit fizzy beholding them, like its synapses were turning into soda—the same way they felt when he came up with an especially insightful Snarl Solution.

Ms. Diamond laid a red-and-white YIELD triangle on top of one stack and said, "That's the last one." She fiddled with a cup attached to a double-helix sculpture made of fused forks, spoons, and knives, and then handed something to the delivery guy and something to Rick.

Rick took it automatically and opened his hand to find a blue-raspberry lollipop. At least he knew that the handing-stuff-to-people technique worked.

Yay! said his stomach. *She's nice. Unwrap that sucker.*

Rick silently told it *not yet* and tucked the lollipop into his front pants pocket. He said, "Your sister is Mrs. Althea Torres, right? Is she ever going to deliver any signs here?"

"My little sister, Althea?" Ms. Diamond said. "Do you know her? No, if you knew her you wouldn't ask if she'd be delivering signs. Chickadee, I may have convinced her to support this project, but that doesn't mean she wants anything to do with it personally. She's too busy for us. Plenty of fires to put out, plenty of things to yell 'Nonsense!' to. But she was nice enough to give us the signs and the help of a work crew from the Department of Transportation to put them up. You artists create your fabulous things, and my sister's crew will make sure they're hung up securely around the city."

Rick turned to the delivery guy. "Could you deliver something to Mrs. Torres for me?"

"Sorry, kid. No unscheduled pickups or drop-offs. In fact, I'd better get to my next stop. You watch out for those purple alligators, now." He chuckled and left.

Ms. Diamond said, "If you have something for my sister, add it to the thank-you cards. I'll be mailing those to her sometime in the next couple of weeks." She pointed to the thick, oversize envelope on the floor next to the as-yet-unpainted pile of signs.

"Oh. Okay."

"Really makes you think of all the good you can do, doesn't it?" Miss Diamond said, looking at the signs.

"Yes," Rick agreed. He was pretty sure they weren't talking about the same good, though.

She said gently, "I couldn't help but notice that you haven't painted anything since you arrived. I know it can be overwhelming. You think you have to do something perfectly the first time or you'll be letting down the greatness you know is within you. Trust me, though—you simply need to take that first brushstroke and get out of your own way. 'If you can dream it, you can do it.'"

Rick knew that quote from the Walt Disney poster outside the school gym. He shook his head. Both Ms. Diamond and Walt Disney were wrong. You couldn't always do it if you could dream it. You had to have other people show up, willing to hear what you had to say.

"Try that first brushstroke," Ms. Diamond encouraged him before going to get more purple paint for Alligator Girl.

Rick bent down and slid his folder into the oversize envelope. Then he turned and faced the room and gave a little shudder. All these poor signs being turned into oddly colored animals. And grinning basketballs. And— was that Scout painting cupcakes on a DO NOT ENTER sign? So many tools for potential Snarl Solutions, ruined.

Mila's smiling face appeared in front of him. "Why aren't you painting yet?" she said. "I picked something for you, I hope you don't mind." She led him over to a STOP sign with a palette of paint laid next to it. "See how mine came out?" she said, displaying her finished art. She'd made a valiant, chubby knight from the number 3 and twined together more dragons, a handful of unicorns, and one flaming orange fox to cover the words *Speed Limit*.

"Very colorful," Rick said.

"Go ahead and do some of your own before Abuelita gets here," she said, handing him a paintbrush.

Rick knelt half-heartedly in front of the STOP sign. There were a few scratches and stains on it, so he dipped his brush in red and carefully painted over them. It took real concentration not to get any on the white parts. The sign looked fresher—happier, even—when he was done. He picked up another brush and dipped it in white to clean up the edges and the letters. Minutes passed.

Someone tapped him on the arm. Abuelita, Ms. Diamond, and Mila were standing behind him, looking over his shoulder at his work. Apparently it was pickup time. Other parents were milling around the room, cooing at their daughters' masterpieces.

"What do you think?" he asked the three of them.

"Hm," said Abuelita. Mila scrunched her face.

Ms. Diamond said, "Well, well, well, look where that first brushstroke took you. Shades of Andy Warhol? Marcel Duchamp? I could tell you had depth. Now, don't forget to sign it." She moved on to the next group.

"Sign it?" Rick looked at Mila.

Mila said, "On the back with a permanent marker. Ms. Diamond says artists should always sign their work. She said we can use our real names or come up with nicknames if we want. I'm using my real name so I can tell people this is how I got my start when I'm a famous artist. You're ... done, right?"

Rick couldn't see anything else to add to the bright STOP sign. "I am." Mila went to go find him a marker as he tipped the sign on one edge. She handed him a black Sharpie.

Rick signed *Richard Stanislav Rusek* before lowering the marker. Then he picked it up again, and when he was sure no one was looking, he crossed out his name and wrote *The Colossus of Roads*. He liked the Colossus name but didn't want to be teased about it.

"My darling chickadees!" Ms. Diamond raised her voice to get the attention of the girls and their parents. "All of the beauteousness you generously created today will be installed around LA to bring joy to those who need more art in their daily lives. Each sign that's finished, please place in that corner. Once I see what we've got, I'll be explaining to some fine employees from the Department of Transportation where to mount your art. So many communities want it! And there are so many signs to be painted that your troop leader and I decided we'll meet not once but twice a week, on Tuesdays and Fridays over the next month, to complete the project. If you can't make both sessions, that's okay. I've also invited several more troops to participate. Help yourselves to lollies on your way out."

Mila had Abuelita snap a picture of her mythical-creature sign with her phone. Abuelita took a shot of Rick's STOP sign as well. Then he and Mila took the two signs and put them in the "finished" corner, and followed Abuelita to her car.

As he opened the rear door, Rick's stomach asked him, *Can you make sure she doesn't swerve anymore?* Before he could speak, Mila asked her grandmother point-blank, "Abuelita, are you going to drive home the way you normally do, or like a really good driver, the way you did on the way here?"

"I am always a really good driver, *mi vida*," Abuelita replied patiently, putting on her gloves. "I can see our Ricardo needs me to drive a certain way, so I do that for him. Other times, the city needs me to drive a certain way, so I do that. You'll understand when you are older." Rick's stomach was relieved to hear it was going to be treated to another paranormally gliding ride.

Feeling less panicked about the drive, Rick now noticed that there was a chunky, chrome-plated radio with a small microphone mounted on top of Abuelita's dashboard and asked her about it.

"It's a ham radio. You've seen the one I have at home, haven't you?" He had. It was parked on a small doily-covered end table in the living room. That one was bigger, though, with knobs the size of hockey pucks and twice as many gauges and switches as this one. He'd heard her chatting on it a few times. "I use my radios to talk to my friends around the city. Right now, though, I'm in the mood for driving music." She clicked on the car's FM radio and electric guitar, bass, and drums filled the car.

It was smooth sailing again as Abuelita sang along with the Rolling Stones. When they got out of the car, Mila tugged on Rick's shirtsleeve. "Something about having you in the car fixed Abuelita."

He held up one arm and flexed his biceps. "In a world where cars need to be driven properly, Rick Rusek makes it happen," he said. Then he unflexed. If only that were true. All he'd done this afternoon was stick his Snarl Solutions in an envelope that would take weeks to reach the busy Mrs. Torres. That wasn't going to protect the good things in his family's life right now. He was back to square one.

→ → →

That night at dinner, Dad asked how the Girl Scout meeting had gone. "What was Anna Diamond like? Did she seem legendary?"

"The meeting was okay, and Ms. Diamond was nice. She let everyone have lollipops," Rick said. He took a mouthful of the lentil stew Mom had served and then wished he hadn't. But he didn't want to complain. Mom looked like she'd had the kind of day where a compliment would go over a lot better than a complaint. "Mmm, this is different," he made himself say. "What is a lentil, anyway?"

Who cares what a lentil is—it's awful! Tell her, or she's going to make it again, his stomach said.

"It's a legume, like a bean," she said. "Do you like it? Each serving cost pennies to make."

"Mmm," Rick said again, swigging some water to get the stew down.

Dad ate a spoonful. Rick could tell by his face that his stomach was making similar comments to him. Dad said, "Anything to go with it? Some bread?"

"Nope, it's a one-dish meal," Mom said. "I got the idea to start making more one-dish vegetarian meals for us. Nutritious and cost-effective." She put her own spoonful in her mouth. After she chewed, she said, "Too bad I started with this one. Are you two actually enjoying it, or trying to spare my feelings?"

"I love you, darling," said Dad.

"I love you too, Mom. Best mom ever," said Rick.

"There's my answer," Mom said. "Darn it. Maybe if I mixed in some leftover slices of kielbasa and cooked it a little longer?"

"Whatever you want to do," Dad said. "Have I told you lately how much I love you? But I would also like to point out that we have cheese and tortilla chips and we could make some nachos out of that instead. Throw some olives on it and voilà, vegetarian one-dish meal. Did I mention that I can prepare this delicious meal while you put your feet up?"

Mom smiled at that, but it was a fleeting smile, chased

right off her face by a sigh. "We can make it together," she said. "Rick, go warm up the couch for us. It's going to be a nachos-in-front-of-mindless-television night."

The nachos were good. The night was not. While his parents cleaned up the dishes, Rick could hear their stressed whispers. Dad offered to look for another graphic design job. Mom said that without his help, she couldn't run Smotch. Then they talked about how much they could cut back, using lots of words like *cancel* and *eliminate* and *tighten*. It sounded like legume-based meals were the beginning of lots of unwelcome changes.

YOU'LL BE SAFE WITH ME

THREE DAYS LATER, at the Herreras' kitchen table, Mila asked, "You're coming with me today, right?" Daniela was with them, singing a song mostly made up of the word *no*.

"Where?" Rick asked.

"To Ms. Diamond's house. You had fun last time, didn't you? And you being in the car will make Abuelita drive so well we'll be on time again. Daniela, try singing this instead—Meeee-laaaa, I loooove youuuu."

Daniela giggled and repeated, "Noooo-noooo, no nooooo noooo!" using the same tone and rhythm.

"*No* must be a fun word to learn to say," Rick observed. "And no, I wasn't planning on coming today." He still hadn't come up with any new ideas on how to help Smotch, so his mood was not the best.

"But look." Mila had Abuelita's phone and started swiping the screen. "Some of our signs are already up. Don't they look amazing?" She showed him a series of smiling cupcakes, basketballs, and tigers lined up along a road median. Then she scrolled to a photo of a damaged park fence to which four painted street signs were affixed in a line—the purple alligator, Mila's mythical creatures, a rainbow with pots of gold at either end, and Rick's fresh STOP sign. Mila let out a happy squeak. Rick couldn't help thinking his sign seemed mournfully out of place, stopping nobody and nothing.

"Please?" Mila said.

We've got less than three weeks to hang out with Mila, his stomach said. *I'll be brave again. Let's go and keep her company.*

"Fine," Rick said. "I suppose I must use my Abuelita-fixing power when called upon to do so." He put his pencil to his forehead like an antenna and made a high-pitched *oooo-oooo-OOOOO* noise.

Daniela looked at his antenna-pencil with wide eyes and repeated *"Oooo-oooo-OOOOO"* over and over.

Rick called his mom to get permission. She said, "More painting? With Girl Scouts?" She muttered something about "raising boys" and "full of surprises" and then told him he could go.

→ → →

Once in the carport, Rick's stomach was not quite as confident as it had been inside Mila's town house. It asked, *What if we can't do this? What if Abuelita's driving last time was a fluke?* Rick sent reassuring brain waves its way, but as he climbed with Mila into the giant red car's backseat, he couldn't help wondering: Was he about to embark on a journey with the best driver in LA, or with someone who might hold up traffic for days?

As he and Mila clicked their seat belts into place, he noticed Mila had crossed her fingers on both hands.

Abuelita reached for the glove compartment and snapped on her red leather driving gloves. Mila uncrossed her fingers and nodded at Rick.

"Okay, *chamitos*, here we go!" Abuelita announced.

"What's a *chamito*?" Rick whispered to Mila as Abuelita turned on the ignition.

"*Chamitos* is a Venezuelan word. It means something like 'kiddos,'" she whispered back. And away they went.

Rick's stomach didn't have any comments for him for the next six miles. When they pulled up to the curb in front of Ms. Diamond's house, all it had to say was *Whoa. Too bad there's only one Abuelita.*

They said goodbye to Abuelita and walked inside behind a pair of girls and a mom. Mila's Girl Scout troop leader and assistant were waiting there, along with more adult volunteers and a whole lot more Scouts than last time. "These must be the other troops Ms. Diamond mentioned," Mila said. "Brown vests are Brownies, khaki vests are Cadettes, and green vests are Juniors like me."

Ms. Diamond was handing out smocks. "Should have had these last week, considering the depth and breadth and height of your enthusiasm. Darling chickadees, should you need a theme, your muse today could be 'California Gold.' What makes our state so splendid? You can continue working on individual road signs as we did last week. Or you can band together and collaborate on some monumental art. For something like this one"—she gestured to a green freeway interchange sign big enough for three Girl Scouts to lie down head to toe on it—"you'll have to plan your work and then work your plan together. Now get ready, get set, get making art."

Mila tugged Rick's sleeve. "Want to work on one of the big ones?" she asked.

"No thanks," he said.

"Oh, okay. Well, I want to work on the biggest one of all, so I'd better go grab a spot." The largest road sign was already getting swarmed by keen artists.

Rick went over to the pile of small signs and picked up as many as he could carry. "You'll be safe with me," he told them.

Rick made his way to an unoccupied spot near the double helix of cutlery. He overheard some Scouts discussing whether they should make the state animal (California grizzly), the state bird (California quail), or the state sport (surfing) the center of one of the big signs. He found a Sharpie and wrote *The Colossus of Roads* on the back of each of his signs. Then he dabbed his brush in some black paint and started restoring a SPEED LIMIT 30.

Rick finished two SPEED LIMIT signs and a DO NOT ENTER. Then the girl behind him, who seemed to have a broken volume control, yelled to Ms. Diamond, "Look! What do you think of this fish taco holding a bouquet of

California poppies?" Rick decided he wasn't going to turn around to see which sign had given up its useful face for a taco and some poppies.

Ms. Diamond made appreciative sounds. The girl yelled back, "How do you put these up when they're dry? Glue? Duct tape?"

Rick laughed inwardly at the girl's question, thinking about his ROAD WORK NEXT 5 MILES sign at home and the big nuts and bolts that had been used to secure it to its pole. If people could use duct tape to put up signs, anyone could put up any sign anywhere they wanted to. It'd be chaos.

His brain fizzed. He held his brush still.

Duct tape. It could do practically anything, right? Why couldn't it be used to hang up road signs? Not by everyone in a chaotic, crazy way, no, but how about by a kid with potentially great ideas?

Oooh, he wanted to try it right now and find out. He had the signs. Now he just needed the tape. He looked around for Mila's troop leader and asked her if she had any of the duct tape left from when Mila made her wallet. "I had, like, an . . . art . . . brainstorm," he explained.

"A Scout leader always has duct tape," she said, pointing to a plastic tub with a couple of first-aid kits, duct tape, and other craft supplies, like Elmer's glue, markers, pipe cleaners, and empty toilet-paper rolls. Rick grabbed a roll of black tape and a roll of red, his mind racing. When he'd looked up Yum Num Donuts online, he thought he'd seen a few of the reasons why traffic so often got snarly here.

He slid the duct-tape rolls onto his arm like bracelets. He found Ms. Diamond and asked her, "Is it okay if I look around your backyard? For art inspiration?" Mila had told him that the fenced-in yard was way bigger than you could see from the road, a whole field of sculpture armadillos, sunflowers, cactuses, and windmills. He was sure he could make it down the street to Yum Num Donuts and duct-tape his signs in place in less time than it would take him to wander around this wonderland of weirdness.

"Of course." She waved breezily toward a sliding glass door. "May you find inspiration in my humble creations to create your own expression of greatness."

"Thank you," he said. He skipped back to the double helix to sort through his stack of signs and selected six he knew he needed, including his two freshly painted SPEED LIMIT signs. He hugged the signs to his chest and casually backed toward the glass door, watching for any suspicious attention from Ms. Diamond or the Scouts, but no faces turned his way. Rick ducked out, as ready as he'd ever been to express his greatness.

→ → →

When he crept back in through the sliding door, Rick was flushed with pride. Things had gone amazingly, and the duct tape had worked like a charm. He had worried that someone might stop and ask him what he was doing, but no one had asked him a thing. The toughest part was darting across the busy street to put some of the signs on the other side.

What he'd done was simple. He'd used a milk crate from a pile he'd found in the alley next to Yum Num Donuts to stand on to boost his height, and taped his signs over the signs that were already there. He increased the speed limit in one section, decreased it in another, and clarified No Parking zones and which lanes were right-turn only. Not everyone had to notice his changes for them to work. If his signs changed the behavior of a few drivers, their behavior should change a few more, who'd influence a few more, until, *click-click-click*, a cascade of good-driving dominoes would keep the pattern going.

He returned to his stash of signs, relieved to see no one had taken any. Ms. Diamond waved at him from her desk. "I hope you found what you were looking for out there."

"Thanks, it was pretty much perfect," Rick answered. When she beamed, he realized she was talking about her metal sculptures. No harm done complimenting her art, he supposed, even though he didn't quite understand why art in general was considered interesting or valuable. It mostly sort of sat there.

It's good at holding lollipops, his stomach suggested.

Mila came over to him with a yellow-soaked paintbrush. She glanced down at his DO NOT ENTER and his remaining stack of unpainted signs.

"You've only painted one? Does it take you a really long time to decide what to do?" Mila asked.

How to answer that? "I guess so. I think the signs deserve lots of careful decision-making," he said.

"Oh, okay. Come see ours!" She led him over to the biggest sign.

The girls had covered about half of the sign with paint. They'd daubed on a background of cerulean sky and three sunshine-tipped mountains. At the mountains' base, an ocean spotted with surfers and shark fins lapped against a beach with palm trees. A golden-maned unicorn charged up the side of each mountain.

"I still think we should do a big ol' grizzly bear in the center, saying something," one girl said.

"I think we should do a desert tortoise," another said. "She and the grizzly could be surfing together."

"I don't think we should have any mythical creatures on it," one girl complained. "Unicorns are so not part of what makes California great."

Mila's paintbrush drooped.

Rick took a closer look at Mila's section. The unicorns had shining eyes and playful smiles, somehow looking both impressively realistic and appealingly cartoony.

"Those unicorns are the best part," Rick said. Mila stood slightly taller.

Ms. Diamond called, "Nearly time to start cleaning up, darlings. Don't worry, your art will have plenty of time to bloom and fill the empty spaces." She addressed the girls gathered around Mila's sign. "I heard a fair amount of discussion here, but not much agreement. It can be hard to collaborate when it comes to creativity, but trust me, trust me, trust me, it is worth trying. When minds and hearts and paintbrushes come together in pursuit of a grand goal, whooo!" She shook her hands like she'd burned them. "Watch out!"

Mila took her paint-filled palette and tugged Rick's shirt so he'd follow her back over to his own sign pile. She said, "If you tell me what you'd like to do, I can help you at least get started on another one before we have to clean up." She knelt down in front of his stack and gently took a STOP HERE ON RED off the top.

"Oh. Um. See, well...," Rick said, sliding the duct-tape rolls off his arm and rotating them back and forth between his hands.

"I know it's not easy to work with other people," Mila said. "It also must feel weird to be the only boy here. But I promise I won't make fun of your ideas." She offered him a brush.

He put down the tape, accepted the brush, and sat cross-legged next to her. He looked at the sign, dipped the brush in white, and cleaned up part of the smog-dulled background. There, that was better.

"Really?" Mila asked, then covered her mouth with her hand. "Sorry. I mean, okay." She dipped her brush in white, too, and cleaned up another section. Rick got some black and made the *H* in *Here* as clear-edged as he could.

"What's up with that duct tape?" Ms. Diamond asked from behind them. Rick turned to give it to her, and she waved it away. "No, chickadee, show me the art you wanted to make with it."

He looked down at the sign. He peeled off a scrap of black tape and stuck it in the middle of the *O* of *Stop* like an eyeball. Ms. Diamond still seemed to be waiting, so he tore off three skinny strips and added eyelashes to the *O*. It gazed up at him in wonder.

Mila covered her mouth again, but Ms. Diamond nodded. "Surrealist? Postmodernist? I'm so glad you were able to join our group." She handed them each a lollipop. "Looking forward to seeing what cleverness appears next week."

"Can I take some signs home with me to keep? They're so cool," Rick said. If his duct-tape solution worked the way he hoped it would, maybe he could somehow duct-tape more signs to save Smotch. He was going to ask his dad to get him some yellow, red, white, black, green, and orange duct tape for that boat project. It felt good to have the glimmer of a plan.

"You're not the first one who's asked me that, but no, not yet. It's not fair to the other Scouts. I want to make sure everyone gets a chance to create"—she looked down at the STOP eyeball—"whatever their hearts desire. Let's talk again if we have leftovers at the end."

Rick tapped his fingers on a tape roll. He didn't have that kind of time. Smotch needed help now.

Abuelita strolled up and asked, "So, did you start making something good?"

Mila glanced at Rick to see what he'd say. "I think I did," he answered.

"Me too," Mila said, smiling.

→ → →

Rick stared at the radio over his cereal spoon. Over the long Labor Day weekend he'd checked the digital maps on the traffic-alert websites and seen that the traffic on his improved section of Balboa Boulevard was moving smoothly. But now it was Tuesday and rush hour—the true test. He'd logged on to his computer first thing this morning to see if the color was closer to red or green. It had been as green as green M&M's with seaweed salad on top.

Blech, his stomach had commented.

Now the radio announcer's smooth, matter-of-fact voice was listing the morning's traffic snarls and hot spots. Twice now, Rick had heard him say, "The Balboa entrance to the One-Eighteen reports no problems." That was radio-announcer-speak for "Congratulations, Rick! Your signs made things better."

Rick let out a giggle. He'd done it. His Snarl Solution had really worked. This must have been how the Colossus of Rhodes felt when conquering Greece! Wait, was that what the person the Colossus statue was modeled on did? He hadn't paid such great attention to that professor. He made a mental note to look it up.

"Keep your mouth closed when you chew. And what are you giggling about?" Mom asked. "You know I don't like being kept out of a joke."

"Yes, Rick, share," Dad chimed in through a mouthful of cornflakes.

Rick swallowed and said, "I was just thinking about something funny that happened at Ms. Diamond's."

"Something funny happened with Mila's troop? Tell us," Mom said. "I could use a laugh. I haven't seen you so tickled since... Hold on, buster, you had better not be planning any pranks around here. I will not be laughing if I find a garter snake in my yogurt container again."

Rick felt another giggle rising but forced it down. "I can't explain. You kind of had to be there."

"Oh, you." Mom finished her cereal and pushed back from the table. "I guess I'll assume you know better than to sneak more snakes into this house. That goes for lizards, too." She ruffled his hair and smiled. "But it's nice to see you happy. Who knew tagging along with Girl Scouts was going to be so good for you?" She looked at Dad. "I bet if your parents had signed you up for Scouts, you wouldn't have taught your son that giving his mom a wild reptile disguised as a nice snack was a funny prank to pull."

"He was such a cute garter-snake snack, wasn't he?" Dad said. "And you laughed like mad after you finished screaming."

"I've never opened another yogurt without cringing first." She smiled one of those fleeting smiles and then let out a giant sigh. "We're off to face another day. And those roads."

As Rick carried his cereal bowl to the sink, Dad said,

"Your mother and I want to hear more about why this art project is so interesting to you and how we might find more activities like it, not to mention how on earth you find Abuelita's driving better than ours. I've seen her, Rick. She makes it impossible for anyone to go faster than about fifteen miles an hour."

"She doesn't drive that way for me," Rick said. "Maybe it's some magic spell. Speaking of Abuelita, could we invite the Herreras for dinner soon? To thank them for being such great neighbors?"

Dad said, "Not this week, Roo." The nickname didn't bug Rick this time. Nothing could bug him. He was a kangaroo on a mission. "We're drumming up some new business. There's a potential client your mom and I are trying to land, and we've got some serious work to do."

"Who's the potential client?" Rick asked.

"Warner Brothers Studio, Burbank," Dad said. "They've got big bucks to spend on catering."

Burbank was on the opposite end of the Valley from their house. They could take either surface streets or freeways to get there. "I'll help you map out the perfect route tonight."

"That'd be great," Dad said, and went to brush his teeth.

Rick checked the Smotch calendar that his mom kept mounted near their front door and saw two upcoming events with long-standing clients in the Valley: a church and a state college. He and his dad had mapped the routes long ago, and Rick knew their traffic challenges. He wished he could tell his parents that his Snarl Solution had worked, but their first instinct might be to march him over to Balboa Boulevard to take things down. Nope. First he had to figure out where to get more signs and how to teleport himself around LA to duct-tape traffic into perfection for Smotch. Then they would see what an ingenious contribution he could make to the family fortune and be on board.

SPEED LIMIT UNICORN

ON THE WAY to school, Rick scouted out every likely-looking heap of junk on his walk for more forgotten road signs. There was a depressing number of heaps of junk, one of them guarded by two protective pit bulls. And there was a depressing number of road signs: none.

He was reluctantly coming around to the idea that he was going to have to steal signs from Ms. Diamond. He wished his parents hadn't raised him to know right from wrong, because this definitely fell on the side of wrong. But, he argued with his uncomfortable conscience, it was going to make something else right. Plus, the signs were recycled materials, and he'd be recycling them to a new purpose that would bring joy to Los Angeles, just like Ms. Diamond and the Girl Scouts wanted him to. He kept throwing justifications at his conscience, which would catch them, examine them, and then throw them back, embroidered with the statement *Taking stuff that doesn't belong to you without permission is wrong.*

That afternoon when he climbed into Abuelita's big red car with Mila, he brought Aleks's old extra-big camping backpack with him for sneaking the signs home. His conscience continued to niggle at him to figure out some other way.

"That's a big backpack," Mila said, watching him wedge it down next to his feet. "What's it for?"

Rick touched the backpack's top flap, where Aleks had stitched on a khaki-and-yellow patch stating BE PREPARED. "My brother used it for Boy Scouts," he said. "I thought it'd help me feel ready to work on the Girl Scout project today."

Abuelita did her smooth driving for over half the ride, but then her ham radio crackled to life. "TCD, TCD, speeding motorcycles in Granada Hills, need someone *now* at Jolette near Balboa. I see a group of kids on foot heading toward a crosswalk." Abuelita sucked in her breath and reached to turn off the radio, but then the voice said, "This is an emergency."

Rick could've sworn Abuelita growled. She picked up the mike. "TCD, Meteoro is on it." And she suddenly turned down a side street. Rick's stomach said, *Hey?* Abuelita then swooshed into an alleyway and onto Jolette, pulling in front of two motorcycles. Rick could smell the rubber burning from the motorcycles screeching to a halt. He heard the two riders yelling unpleasant things.

Abuelita drove forward excruciatingly slowly and swervingly. Rick's stomach started to panic, and he scrabbled in the backpack for a double-reinforced bag.

Abuelita then reached a crosswalk and stopped her

car diagonal to it. The motorcyclists tried to get Abuelita's attention. She pointedly ignored them, instead waving and beaming at the children chasing each other across the crosswalk. Once there were no more kids on the sidewalk on either side, she did a slow-motion three-point turn and resumed driving in her smooth and gliding style.

"What was that, Abuelita?" Mila asked.

"Nothing for you to worry about," she said. "Okay back there, Ricardo?"

Rick checked himself out. His stomach was tense, on the verge of ghastlier things, but he wasn't going to die. "Kind of?" he answered, but his stomach was still whimpering when they arrived at Ms. Diamond's house. *What just happened? Who was she talking to? And how do we make sure it never happens again?* Rick didn't have any answers.

As they walked up to the front door, Mila sighed and said, "Guess it was too good to last." She asked if he wanted to work together some more, but he told her he was all set and headed for the pile of unpainted signs. He grabbed another heavy stack—all the signs he'd need to fix his parents' drive to the college, the church, and the movie studio—and added them to the pile he'd safely tucked in his corner last Friday. He slid one inside the camping backpack. His conscience threw a fastball embroidered with *Taking stuff that doesn't belong to you without permission is wrong* into his gut and Rick exhaled with a *whoof* sound.

He took the sign back out and looked over at Ms. Diamond, wondering if she was the type who yelled when she got angry. She was seated in the squeaky chair at her desk with a pencil stuck behind each ear and another between her teeth. She was using yet another pencil to write and then immediately erase things on a piece of paper.

She must have felt his gaze, because she looked up. "Marcel Duchamp!" she slurred around the pencil in her mouth. She removed it and said, "Come on over here, please!"

"It's Rick," he said with as much calmness as he could muster while his stomach shouted *She knows! Run!* He told his stomach to be cool and approached the desk. When he got close, he saw that the pencil behind one of her ears was decorated with saber-toothed cats advertising the La Brea Tar Pits, and the one behind her other ear with jelly-fish advertising the Long Beach Aquarium.

She gave him a friendly smile and said, "Rick it is. How's your painting going? Have time to discuss your artistic vision? I'd much rather talk surrealism with you than keep doing this." She used the pencil in her hand to poke the paper. "Self-explanatory, my foot."

Rick glanced at the paper she'd poked and did a double-take. "Wow! Is that an LADOT work order?" he asked. The LADOT logo, for the Los Angeles Department of Transportation, was at the top of the page, and there was a jagged black *Althea Torres* signature at the bottom. It had spaces demanding lots of measurements and labels, and Ms. Diamond had drawn tiny sketches of Girl Scout signs in the margins.

Ms. Diamond poked the work order again, and Rick saw that it was made up of several papers stapled together. "My sister gave these to me so I can explain to her work crew where our art should go. I filled them out, but she sent some of them back to me after the crew couldn't decipher them, insisting I complete them 'properly.' I'm not clear on what she means. If I want something hung on a fence, I thought I could write *hang it on the fence*—but apparently, in some locations, I need to indicate if the fence runs north to south or east to west, how many feet high and how many feet apart the signs should be hung, and all kinds of other details. It's even more complicated if I want them installed near a road. She says I have to be that specific on all work going forward, and I'm falling way behind. Art's my thing, not paperwork."

"I can help," Rick said, eyes bright. "What are you trying to do with this one?"

Ms. Diamond described cheering up an area where demolition had uglified a neighborhood. Rick asked, "Can we open Google Maps?" gesturing toward her computer. "Tell me the address and how you want things to look."

In a few minutes, Rick was sitting in Ms. Diamond's squeaky chair with the jellyfish pencil in his hand. He translated what Ms. Diamond wanted done into clearly labeled, precise measurements on the papers, detailing how some signs should be bolted to the sides of buildings and chain-link fences, while others needed to be mounted to new metal posts sunk into the ground. "Do you have any more?"

"Well." Ms. Diamond put her hand to her chest. "Yes. Dozens. But I hate to ask you to give up any creative time to help with this."

A girl across the room called out "Help, Ms. Diamond! We're out of red paint!" Ms. Diamond turned, clearly longing to assist with art challenges instead of work orders.

"I don't need that much, um, creative time," Rick said. "And I'd love to help out with something I know I'm good at."

"Marcel—Rick—you are a lifesaver. Here's the deal: Please first go and paint whatever it is you are called to paint today. When you feel you are finished, meet me back here and let's see if we can't forge our way through a few more."

"That's a deal," Rick said. He got up to return to his sign pile to pretend to be creative for a few minutes.

Whew, his stomach said. *I did a good job being cool, didn't I?*

A great job. Rick's brain was fizzing like crazy. Now he didn't have to sneak any signs home. With work orders like these, he could have official crews with the proper tools putting up his Snarl Solutions literally anywhere.

Wait, you're going to fill out some of those work orders with your own ideas? What if the work crew notices? his stomach asked nervously. *I don't want your conscience throwing things at me anymore. This is more serious than your duct-tape experiment.*

Rick sat on the tile floor to shift his signs around. He got a look of astonishment from his one-eyed STOP HERE

ON RED. *I'll be ordering signs painted by a kid to be hung up*, Rick told his stomach. *That's the whole reason for this project.* All he needed to do was make sure every sign he used for his own work orders was one to which he'd added some paint. It'd be its own kind of public art—art that did something important. He decided he couldn't worry about what the work crew might notice. He had to take this chance to save Smotch.

Rick picked up his paintbrush and freshened the colors wherever scratches and scars dimmed a sign's beauty. Then he autographed the back of every new sign *The Colossus of Roads*.

When he got up to find Ms. Diamond and tell her he'd painted as much as he wanted to, he noticed Mila sitting near the freeway painting she'd been working on last time. She was extra still and quiet, but not her normal at-ease-with-quiet quiet. More like a wilted plant. Three older girls were making broad strokes with brown paint, finishing off a giant grinning grizzly bear. His teeth were as big as the girls' hands.

Rick moved to get a better view of the sign and Mila's unicorns. But her unicorns were nowhere to be seen. It looked like they'd been painted over with lifeless brown boulders.

Mila squared her shoulders and picked up a paintbrush and dabbed at a palette, murmuring something Rick didn't catch.

"No, sorry. I already told you we agreed on a plan, and

it's Chompy McChompface here," one girl said matter-of-factly. "If you want to add some redwoods or clouds, we could use more of those."

Mila sat for a minute longer, not painting anything. Then she got up, still holding her paintbrush, and walked to a far corner of the room. She stopped there, stone-faced, looking at the ground.

Rick followed her and stood beside her for a few moments. "Not interested in helping with Chompy McChompface?" he finally asked.

"I'm just going to do my own thing. It's fine," Mila said, shoulders hunching.

"Okay. Glad you're fine. It's a little hard to tell, since you usually have a face that says *I love making art* and right now you have a face that says you want to punch something," Rick said. "Maybe you should try giving me a big chompy smile and then I'll believe you."

Mila gave him a still-stony look.

He pulled his lips back and bared his teeth in a wide grimace. "It'sh eashy, shee?" Then a stream of drool let loose from his bottom lip, making it all the way to his shirt. "Whoopsh." He wiped his chin with the back of his hand. "That wasn't as attractive as it could have been."

Mila tried to cover up her smile, but the stone had definitely cracked. Then she sighed. "All the girls from my troop are working on small signs, and I really, really wanted to decorate a big sign with some mythical creatures. They're the best thing I can draw. They're how I can bring joy to Los Angeles. I'm supposed to be a sister to every Girl Scout, and they're supposed to be sisters to me, but I find it so hard to speak up with people I don't know." She added under her breath, "Especially people I'm not sure I like all that well."

"Maybe you could join a different group?" He started walking around to see what other projects were under way. Mila followed him. None of the big signs had even a hint of myth about them (although Rick didn't hate the one that featured a giant hamburger under two crossed palm trees). They ended up at the small pile of signs that hadn't been claimed.

"Well, I'm out of amazing ideas," Rick said. He looked longingly at Ms. Diamond's desk. *Technically, I'm full of amazing ideas, but none of them involves Girl Scouts.*

"Oh, okay," Mila said. Her chin was starting to hunch in on her neck as well.

"Wait, I just remembered I forgot to tell you my best idea of all!" Rick could not focus on making a work order until Mila put her I-love-making-art face back on. "You should paint a whole bunch of these small signs, because with enough mythical small signs, you can combine them to make one ginormous, mythically mythtastic sign."

"How do I do that?" Mila asked.

"Naturally, you use a mythical type of glue. Like . . . centaur cement."

"Hm. I don't think Ms. Diamond has any centaur

cement in her supply closet," Mila said, her eyes crinkling at the corners.

He had a thought that seemed sure to cheer her up. "You didn't let me finish the best part of the best idea of all," Rick said, grabbing some small signs and taking them to his corner. "Before we locate the centaur cement, I will paint something amazing on the top part of these, and then you will paint something mythical below. We'll plan our work and work our plan. For instance..." He pointed to a SPEED LIMIT 65 sign, picked up a paintbrush with a flourish, dipped it in black paint, and meticulously smoothed it over the letters *S-P-E-E-D* and *L-I-M-I-T* until they shone glossily. "There it is, my masterpiece. What do you have to add to that?"

Both Mila's eyes and her lips were crinkled now. She knelt down next to him and used sure strokes of white, yellow, and blue, until she'd covered the number 65 with the regal face and horn of a unicorn.

"I dub this work of genius SPEED LIMIT UNICORN," Rick said solemnly.

Mila cracked up. "Let's try another one."

Rick chose a SPEED LIMIT 55 sign and said, "Get ready. More artistic brilliance is about to be unleashed." Once again he traced carefully over the words with black paint. "What do you have to match that?"

"Got it," Mila answered, diving in with her own paintbrush to cover the numbers with a fire-spouting red dragon in flight. "Here's SPEED LIMIT DRAGON."

"My amazingness clearly inspires you, doesn't it?" Rick grabbed a YIELD. "But what could you possibly do to improve this?" He started tracing the letter Y with black paint. They ended up going back and forth, until they had YIELD TO HIPPOGRIFFS, PEGASUS CROSSING, PHOENIXES RIGHT LANE ONLY, NO PARKING EXCEPT MERMAIDS, and another SPEED LIMIT UNICORN, this last one with a unicorn in profile clearly running at top speed, mane rippling in the wind.

Ms. Diamond passed by, setting down a fresh stack of small signs. "Didn't I promise you there was magic in collaboration? Keep it up, keep it up," she encouraged as she moved on to the next group.

Mila whispered, "She likes everything anyone creates, doesn't she? Even if it's a duct-tape eyeball. Oh!" She put her hand to her mouth. "No offense."

"Believe me, none taken," Rick said. The best part about his eyeball and eyelashes was how easily they could be peeled off.

"Want to do a few more?" Mila said, reaching for the fresh stack. She was firmly back in I-love-making-art mode.

Rick couldn't deny the call of the work orders any longer. "I am out of artiness at this point, and I promised Ms. Diamond I'd help her with some paperwork," he said. "Those are all yours."

He stepped over PEGASUS CROSSING to get to Ms. Diamond's desk. He looked at the ridiculous sign, then back at Mila, her tongue poking out of the corner of her mouth as she unicorned up a railroad crossing sign. *Thank goodness road signs are made by machines, not artists,* he thought. But he admired the curve of the flying horse's wings, and didn't feel that much of an urge to wipe the paint clean.

Rick met up with Ms. Diamond at her desk and eagerly asked for more work order directions. She showed him a pad of paper on which she'd listed ten different addresses and which Girl Scout designs she wanted mounted at each one.

"What if I try filling out a few more based on this list and show them to you?" Rick said. "That way, you're free to help the Scouts."

"You do that and I'm getting out my special stash of Blow Pops for your reward."

Rick refreshed Google Maps and began filling out the work orders with more labels and measurements. After he showed her the first two completed orders, Ms. Diamond told him he was a godsend and ducked into her kitchen, returning with the promised bubble-gum-centered lollipops. She asked if he'd mind doing as many as he could stand. "Once they're done, we simply stack up the signs near the garage door with the appropriate work order clipped to the top sign for each location." She showed him a box of large black binder clips. "I've gathered a few piles already. The Department of Transportation delivery truck will be by to pick them up later."

By the time Abuelita arrived, he'd finished work orders for Ms. Diamond's ten locations, plus filled out three more, so his Colossus signs would be put up on the routes to the college, the church, and the movie studio, which he and his dad had mapped out last night. He'd clipped the orders to the pile of signs, hiding his underneath Ms. Diamond's.

Being able to summon up his talent and seize this chance to help his family made him feel like he'd grown six inches. He'd also blown a bunch of noteworthy bubble-gum bubbles. He was buzzing with so much glee on the way out, his stomach had to prompt him three times before he noticed: *Ask Abuelita to keep me in mind on the drive home.* He did.

Abuelita smiled and assured him, "*Sí*, Ricardo, I'm keeping you in mind while I drive. I keep all the children of Los Angeles in my mind when I drive."

Does that mean we're safe? his stomach asked uncertainly. Rick wasn't sure what it meant. He looked at Mila, who gave a hopeful shrug. He silently told his stomach, *Let's believe that it does.*

He turned out to be right.

FOCUS ON THE HAPPY THINGS IN LIFE

RICK FOUND IT impossible to try to learn anything the next morning in first-block social studies. The Department of Transportation crew must have worked overtime the night before. According to the digital maps on the internet and the radio reports, as of this morning, traffic along the routes of his three Colossus "art installations" was moving smoothly. Maybe the crew was too tired to notice, or maybe they didn't care, but he hadn't been caught. Rick's stomach was extremely happy. And today, his folks were catering a lunch buffet at the state college and dropping off food for a fellowship dinner meeting at the church. He couldn't wait to talk to them and find out how the traffic had been.

Rick bounced his leg up and down, not absorbing anything his teacher was saying about Christopher Columbus. He stared at the poster near the door: "If you think you can, or if you think you can't, you're right."—Henry Ford.

You know it, Henry, he said to himself.

He'd tell Mom and Dad tonight. They'd be so relieved

to know their business was going to be okay, not to mention impressed at how their youngest son had made it happen. Sure, his brothers, Aleks and Thomas, could drive and cook and serve, but had they ever turned miles of roadway green before?

The bell rang. Rick gathered his stuff in a happy haze. He high-fived the Henry Ford poster on the way out of the room.

At lunch, Rick looked around for Tennis but didn't spot him. He picked an empty seat and heard the students around him discussing which Lakers team member was the best of all time. One kid kept interjecting jokes that got the whole table laughing. Rick wished he understood enough of the conversation to join in the laughter and add some comments of his own, but he heeded Tennis's advice and kept quiet. He decided to look up the Lakers broadcast schedule that night and start studying up on the players' stats.

Please do, his stomach encouraged him. *You need more somebodies to talk to at school than your digestive system.*

But you're such a super conversationalist, Rick thought, telling it not to worry. The only changes coming his way were positive ones. His parents would have a thriving business. He'd be able to keep spending afternoons at the Herreras'. And he'd make new friends. He tossed out his trash and fist-bumped a poster of Eleanor Roosevelt assuring him, "The future belongs to those who believe in the beauty of their dreams." He was starting to appreciate why the school hung these inspirational sayings from every available surface. Eleanor Roosevelt and Henry Ford were right on the money.

→ → →

Mom picked up Rick from the Herreras' early again.

"Mom!" he said as they walked from one front door to another, Rick bouncing on the balls of his feet. "How was your day? Great, right? Is Dad home early, too?"

"Today was good enough," Mom said. "Dad's doing the dinner drop-off." Once inside the house, she opened the pantry and sighed as she pondered its contents.

Rick said, "Your day was good enough? Are you sure it wasn't closer to great? Bet your drive to the college has never been better." He decided to restrain himself from blurting out the great news about his Snarl Solutions until Dad got home, but that didn't mean he couldn't fish for a few compliments first.

Mom tilted her head. "Now that you mention it, it was problem-free. I wish I could say that about everything else."

Rick was surprised she wasn't in higher spirits. Maybe one smooth drive wasn't enough to get her feeling optimistic again. "Are you worried about landing that new client?" he asked.

"Dad told you about that?" Mom asked. "Yes, actually, it's been on my mind all day. We're catering a meeting for some movie-studio executives in a little over a week, and if it goes well, they might want to offer us a permanent gig on the studio lot serving lunch three times a week. The pay is terrific."

"That sounds completely great. Maybe famous actors will end up eating your kielbasa and recommend you to other famous actors, and you'll end up playing a kielbasa cook in a blockbuster movie," Rick said, starting to bounce on the balls of his feet again.

Mom snorted. "Ha!" She picked up a bag of dried black beans and another of rice. "Don't think I'm cut out to be an actress. I'll be happy if this first job goes off without a hitch. The odds aren't good. They've moved the location and the time for our trial run. To get there in time to set up and serve a very early lunch, we'll need to get over the hill at rush hour." With that last sentence, her head dipped and her voice took on the tone of someone saying "The end of the world is nigh." She dumped a cup of beans and some spices into the pressure cooker.

Rick stopped bouncing. Getting "over the hill" meant taking the 405 Freeway over Sepulveda Pass, up through the Santa Monica mountains and down the other side. His stomach did a slow roll as he imagined the 330,000 cars oozing through there on an average workday. It was one of the most scraped-skateboarder-red sections of not only the 405, but also all of LA. The traffic jams there were considered by experts to be unfixable. In fact, whenever the Department of Transportation tried to fix the gridlock by adding more lanes, journalists predicted construction-triggered traffic nightmares bad enough to be called the Carpocalypse and Carmageddon.

Well. If his parents needed to get over the hill, then that was what had to happen. Rick would have to put together a seriously colossal new Snarl Solution for this. "Excuse me, Mom. There's a project I need to do work on," he said. He needed to study Sepulveda Pass right now. It looked like he'd have to put off explaining how he'd saved Smotch until he'd really saved it.

Mom nodded. Then the bag of rice ripped and spilled on the floor. "Perfect," she said, and went to get the dustpan. Rick bent over to start scooping up rice with his hands, but Mom waved him toward his room. "I've got this. You work on your project."

"Everything's going to be okay, Mom," Rick said.

She gave him one of those fleeting smiles. "Sure it is."

→ → →

Rick stared at 360-degree views of Sepulveda Pass online. He hoped his brain would start to fizz with the perfect solution, but this puzzle was proving much trickier than most. He could see changes he could make that would probably improve things, but maybe not enough. Rick tried to recapture the certainty he'd felt when high-fiving the Henry Ford poster at school. "If I think I can, I can," he said to his pad of graph paper. It didn't disagree.

He heard Dad come home and proudly announce that traffic on the way to church had been so smooth he'd been early for the dinner drop-off. His stomach said, *See, you know what you're doing.*

That night at dinner, he told his parents he'd become a loyal Lakers fan. "Preseason games start this month. I want to see if LeBron James can top his free-throw percentage from last season." He figured he'd start trying out some of the lingo on Mom and Dad before doing it at school.

"Oh dear. Lakers games." Mom looked at Dad before she said, "We need to tell you something. We decided to cancel our cable today. So...no live games. But on the upside: fewer scary news reports, fewer mindless, time-wasting shows."

"Aw, man," Rick said. "I mean, okay." There was no point in complaining. This was temporary. He would fix Sepulveda first; then his parents would have enough money for cable again, and he'd be able to join lunchtime discussions at Eleanor Roosevelt Elementary.

"We decided renting movies at the library would do it for us," Dad said with false cheerfulness. Rick knew Dad would miss his cable news. In fact, Rick knew all three of them would miss the fun of mindless television nights.

"We'll get the cable back when you get that movie studio contract, right?" Rick asked.

"Oh, let's give this a real try first," Mom said. "Homes without the constant barrage of commercials from cable TV are supposed to produce more grounded children."

She was really committed to making it seem like they were removing good things from their life due to sound parenting, not money problems.

→ → →

Friday afternoon at the Herreras', Abuelita came in from the living room, where she'd been watching television, and said, "No Girl Scout meeting today, *chamitos.*"

Rick looked up from playing tug-of-war with a paper towel with Daniela. "Was it canceled?" he asked.

Mila looked up from her homework. "Why'd they cancel it? Will they reschedule it?"

"No, it's not canceled, but there's no getting there. Listen." Abuelita stood in the doorframe between the two rooms and used the remote to turn up the volume on the TV.

"Our studio has gotten a lot of calls about Balboa Boulevard. Since early this afternoon, the traffic there near the 118 has been stopped dead in both directions. There are no accidents or construction reported; however, people have been stuck for hours, and it's showing no signs of improving. If anyone has details about this situation, text your tips to us."

A reporter then interviewed a lady in a minivan. She'd gotten out of her car to use a bathroom and come back to realize things were still not moving, so she'd ended up walking away to get a couple of convenience-store hot dogs. When she returned, not a single car had moved a single inch. They cut to a shot of a couple of gentlemen selling a wheelbarrow-full of water bottles and oranges to thirsty drivers. Another guy with an empty wheelbarrow was trying to appeal to bored drivers with a cardboard sign that said TAKE A RIDE IN THE WHEELBARROW $1.

Abuelita shut the TV off and flapped one hand. "*Phsst.* Another crazy afternoon in the City of Angels."

"Aw!" said Mila. "I was looking forward to painting today."

The hair on the back of Rick's neck stood up. He felt a sudden need to check on his duct-taped signs. "That doesn't sound so bad. Let's go anyway." He tried to sound casual, but his voice squeaked on the last word.

Abuelita said, "'Doesn't sound so bad,' Ricardo? It broke some kind of record!"

Something was telling Rick he absolutely had to check on his signs, right now. He knew there was a roundabout way to get there from when he'd looked up the location of Yum Num Donuts online. "What about if we went south and then east around the San Fernando Mission instead of our usual route? If we left right now, we could park a few blocks away and walk and still make it in plenty of time."

Are you sure about this? his stomach squeaked, like his voice just had. Rick shifted in his chair and mentally begged his innards to work with him.

Mila added her voice to Rick's. "Could we try going that different way? And you could stay and wait for us and get something at Yum Num Donuts. You know how much you love their apple fritters. Please?" Somehow she made her eyes look like a puppy's.

"Please?" Rick echoed.

Abuelita looked at them both and then raised her arms to heaven. "Does every grandmother fall for a child's 'please'? Fine, we'll try it. But if it looks like we're going to get caught up in the mess, I'm turning around. And I will get a fritter." She smacked her lips. "Yum Num does make the best apple fritters."

The drive in this new direction made Rick's stomach moan, even though Abuelita was doing her hit-every-light-while-it's-green trick. Rick wasn't sure how much of his queasiness came from the traffic and how much came from the feeling something bad had happened. He tried to hide the fact that he was slipping a double-reinforced bag out of his backpack, but Mila saw and shot him a pity-ing look, mouthing, *Thanks for doing this with me.* He was relieved when they found a parking space three blocks away from Yum Num Donuts and he was able to tuck the unused bag away.

"We're a little early. Why don't you come with me before we go to the artist's house," Abuelita said. "I'll buy you both an apple fritter."

Do I like those? his stomach asked faintly. *I bet I like those. Ask me when I can think about it better.*

As they approached the bakery on foot, Rick shaded his eyes from the intense sunshine of a Southern Califor-nia afternoon. They crossed the sea of still-unmoving cars that was Balboa Boulevard. He saw that his duct-taped signs had been seriously messed with. Five had been switched to the opposite side of the street from where he had placed them. One had been thrown into a dusty ditch near the sidewalk.

Rick made a strangled noise and went to rescue the dusty sign from the ground. The front had been graffitied with purple paint.

"Yuck, what a mess," Mila said. "Why do that? It doesn't even look like anything but a dripping blob. We should bring it with us to Ms. Diamond's house and fix it up."

Rick held the sign flat with clenched fists and made a new, more-strangled noise in response. This sign already *had* been fixed up—perfectly. His face got hot. Someone messing with his signs felt like someone messing with his skin.

Abuelita felt Rick's forehead. "You feeling okay, Ricardo?"

"No. Not okay. This is wrong," he said.

She rubbed his back. "Can't let vandalism get you too far down or you'll never get up again. Breaking things and spray-painting them is a full-time job for some hee-haws around here. Let's go inside and focus on the happy things in life, like fritters. Also, I need the restroom." She went into the Yum Num Donuts entrance, which was crowded with other people ready to focus on their own happy, sprinkle-covered, chocolate-frosted, jelly-filled things.

Mila followed, looking over her shoulder at Rick when he didn't move.

"I need a minute," he said.

She said, "Okay. I'll see you in line."

Rick loosened his grip on the sign to check the damage. Not only had someone spray-painted a drippy purple blob on the front, but when he flipped it over, he saw they'd stuck stickers of purple octopuses over the back. Where he'd signed it with his Sharpie, someone had sprayed an inexplicable epithet over the name Colossus of Roads. It said *SPLAT*. He ripped off the stickers and put them in the trash.

The duct tape was still in place, but the sticky bits were now plastered with sand and dirt. This sign couldn't be rehung. Rick tenderly placed it back down, telling it, "Wait for me here. Right now, I need to put your friends back where they belong." The signs wouldn't work as well with one missing, but he had to do what he could.

He found a milk crate and ran from signpost to signpost, repairing the damage. Just like last time, no drivers paid him any attention. He found that his duct tape was still plenty sticky. Correcting the five signs went more quickly than setting them up in the first place, because he didn't have to wait for traffic to slow for him to cross the street. These other five signs were definitely the work of the same vandals: they may not have had blobs spray-painted on the front, but the back of each was coated with octopus stickers and the word *SPLAT*.

Rick felt more human after this act of restoration. He walked under DON TS: THE ONLY THING MISSING IS "U" and joined Abuelita and Mila inside, wiping his face with the corner of his shirt. The smells of yeasty dough and sugary glazes wafted around him.

Mila awkwardly patted his shoulder. "I wish Ms. Diamond could meet the jerks who did that and show them how to make old signs beautiful instead of ruining them," she said. "She'd say 'Make art everywhere you go and find art everywhere you look' that way she does and make them understand."

Rick nodded. If Mila had replaced the word *art* with *Snarl Solutions*, they were in complete agreement, he figured.

They made it to the counter and Abuelita ordered three fritters. But when Abuelita opened the bag to offer him one of the grease-paper-wrapped goodies, his stomach let out distressed bubbles and squeaks, moaning, *I wish I wanted to eat that soooo much, but I'm too upset*. Both Mila and Abuelita gave him a pitying look when he said, "Can we save mine for later?" Rick tried hard to appreciate that the only thing missing at Yum Num Donuts today wasn't him, but that was the best he could do for now.

NOT YOUR ONLY TALENT

BACK OUT ON the sidewalk, Rick collected the sabotaged sign and tucked it under his arm, impatient to restore it again. In fact, once he'd cleaned it up, maybe he'd design a work order to fix this section of Balboa permanently. It'd be much harder for hee-haws and jerks to rip down road signs fastened with solid Department of Transportation nuts and bolts.

After walking with him and Mila to Miss Diamond's house, Abuelita decided to go for a stroll and drop in on one of her friends. At Ms. Diamond's, fewer Girl Scouts than normal had made it, but the ones who were there were painting like mad. Rick and Mila headed toward the double helix where they'd been working last time. "Maybe we can work together to help fix that poor thing," Mila said as Rick put down the vandalized sign.

"Thanks, but I've got it," he responded.

"Oh. Okay," she said, her voice tinged with disappointment.

"A nice surprise arrived today!" Ms. Diamond announced to the group. "An extra delivery of freeway signs!" She waved to a stack. None of them approached the dimensions of the grizzly sign, but a few were sizable. Rick knew what would make Mila smile. He hurried over and said, "I'll take two of the biggest ones you've got."

"All yours, chickadee," she said.

Rick dragged the signs back to Mila and said, "All yours, mythical-creature painter." He'd imagined she would clap her hands with quiet delight. Instead, she was searching around on the floor with a stricken expression.

"Where are the signs I did last time? And the ones we did together?" A dragon and the two SPEED LIMIT UNICORNS were still there, but the rest of them weren't.

Rick scratched his head. He knew he hadn't listed those signs on any work orders. "Ms. Diamond?" he called. "Did you write up plans for more signs to be hung since last week?"

She looked sheepish. "No, I was waiting for you."

Mila's looking so distressed made Rick feel less so. This would be an easy problem to solve. "They're around here somewhere," he assured her. "I'll help you find them."

They walked around the room together, until Mila stopped. Rick looked where she was looking. The older girls who'd taken over the Chompy McChompface sign had finished it with bold white letters at the top: THE SKY'S THE LIMIT. Now they'd turned their attention to some smaller signs. One girl was starting to spread blue paint across NO PARKING EXCEPT MERMAIDS.

Mila didn't look like she could speak, so Rick did it for

her. "Stop that!" he said. "What's wrong with you?" No more vandalizing of signs was happening today if he had anything to say about it.

The girls looked up at him in surprise. "What's the problem?" one asked.

"You can't take my friend's signs and paint over them. Give those back!" He stomped toward them, and the girls scuttled away from him.

"We didn't know these weren't up for grabs," one girl said sulkily.

"Yeah, they looked like mistakes," another said. "Sorry."

Rick didn't bother to reply. He loaded Mila's creature signs onto a drop cloth and dragged them to safety. Mila followed him.

"The paint we use dries pretty quickly, but let's see if it's not too late to wipe it off," Rick said, using the edge of the drop cloth to do exactly that. The blue paint smeared. The mermaid was visible, but in a pale underwater-ish way.

"Well, at least we saved the rest of them," Rick said.

"Thanks," Mila said. Rick could barely hear her.

He handed her a paintbrush and nudged one of the big new signs toward her with his sneaker. "You can't let those hee-haws get you down," he said. "Keep painting. Think about the wise words of Eleanor Roosevelt."

She sat, still and cross-legged, no sign of her I-love-to-make-art face.

Rick sucked in his cheeks to make a super-serious presidential-wife-looking face. "Women are like tea bags—

no one knows how strong they are until you…uh…put them near a plate of cookies?"

"It's 'No one knows how strong they are until they're in hot water,'" Mila whispered.

"No, no, you're quite wrong," Rick said quickly, raising his voice to a falsetto. "I am Eleanor Roosevelt, and I should know my own quotes! Now, young Mila Herrera, get some paint on that paintbrush and keep your eyes on the stars and your feet on the ground!"

"That's Teddy Roosevelt," Mila whispered a tiny bit louder.

"Are you sure? Didn't he say something about not fearing fear itself?" Rick answered, still doing the falsetto.

"That's Franklin Delano Roosevelt," she half announced, half whispered, a ghost of a smile stealing onto her face.

"Sheesh, how's a kid supposed to keep his inspirational quotes straight with all these Roosevelts to keep track of?" he answered in his own voice.

Mila patted her brush timidly on her paint palette. She took in a deep breath and let it out slowly. "Do you ever wonder if your only talent matters at all?"

"Sort of. Mostly I feel like no one wants to know about my only talent because it makes no sense to them. If I were a great basketball player or a straight-A student, I'd get tons of attention, but if I say 'Hey, I understand traffic patterns,' people look at me like I've got ants crawling out of my nose," Rick said.

"Understanding traffic is not your only talent," Mila said. "You're good at making me laugh."

"Oh yeah?" Rick was surprised by how nice that comment made him feel. "How about my art talent? Isn't that also worth mentioning?" He made an extravagant gesture toward their original SPEED LIMIT UNICORN sign.

Mila giggled. "That's exactly what I'm talking about."

"I bet your only talent isn't your mythical-creature painting, either," Rick said.

"No?"

Rick thought about it for a minute, trying to give her a sincere answer. "You have so many different ways of being quiet. Happy quiet, nervous quiet, hardworking quiet, not-minding-other-people-needing-to-be-quiet quiet." He was getting warmed up now. "You have the I'm-making-art-yay quiet, your I'm-really-listening-to-you quiet, and your I'm-pretending-to-be-fine quiet.... There are probably a lot more besides that I'm missing."

Mila smiled and shook her head. "You know what? The sisterhood bond I'm supposed to have with every one of those Girl Scouts? I'm giving it to you instead." She leaned forward and punched Rick on the upper arm.

"Ow!" he said, rubbing it. "What was that for?"

"Sorry," Mila answered, abashed. "I thought that's what sisters are supposed to do with brothers—punch them sometimes. It's what my dad's sister does to him."

"Oh," Rick said, giving his arm one last rub. "Okay. Maybe you can warn me next time so I can brace myself.

You apparently also have the talent to give your friends bruises."

"Well, you have the talent to convince your friend to get back to her painting," Mila said, dabbing her paintbrush on her palette with authority. "I still love doing it, no matter what." She applied a twisty trail of orange scales atop the words *Memorial Freeway* and drifted into a contented silence.

"Good," Rick said sincerely. He got busy collecting the signs he thought would work for his Sepulveda solution. He knew something was missing, but he could prep these signs today and use the weekend to figure out what that was before filling out a work order at the next session. He began retouching the signs, tackling the vandalized sign blob first, removing the duct tape, and obliterating the purple with a thick application of clean, bright white paint. *Take that, purple splats!* his stomach crowed. *Bet they didn't realize this sign was under the protection of the Colossus of Roads.* It was enormously satisfying.

The grizzly girls announced that they were done. Ms. Diamond said, "There's a preschool in Pacoima that's going to appreciate this big bear." She got the dolly, and all the adults in the room helped move the sign to where the delivery guy would come pick it up. As Ms. Diamond passed Rick, she asked him if he had time to help with a few work orders before he had to leave. He surveyed his painting and nodded, then quickly signed the backs with

"The Colossus of Roads." As he approached Ms. Diamond's desk, he was exuding his own Yay-I-don't-have-to-hide-my-talent-right-now quiet.

→ → →

That evening, Dad made popcorn on the stove and put on an Avengers movie he'd borrowed from the library. He and Rick sprawled on the couch and enjoyed the show. Mom, though, stayed hunched over the kitchen table with her calculator the whole time. When she finally got up and came to see if there was any popcorn left, the final credits were rolling. "Darn it, I missed the best part of the day," she said. "We'll do something fun together tomorrow."

Saturday morning, Rick found out what the "something fun" would be: Mom came into his room and woke him up, saying "Rise and shine! Dad has to head to the bank, so it's just you and me for a while. I thought today would be a good day to work on that duct-tape boat you said you were interested in trying out. Where's the tape Dad bought?" She started poking around his room.

Rick rubbed his eyes and stretched. He'd planned to chain himself to his desk and not get up until he'd solved the Sepulveda puzzle. "The regatta thing isn't until October. I'm still not sure about signing up for Cub Scouts."

"Come on. Let's just try making the boat. It'll be fun. I've noticed how happy those art-project outings have made you, and I figured since I haven't been the best company lately, spending some creative time with my favorite Roo would be just what the doctor ordered. Aha!" Mom waved a roll of black tape she found on his desk. "We'll start after breakfast."

She was making an effort to be his regular old mom again, like she wasn't being nibbled inside by constant worry, so Rick didn't have the heart to correct the nickname. "Duct-tape boat-building it is," he said, swinging his feet over the edge of the bed. He supposed he had all weekend to figure out what was missing from his Sepulveda Pass Snarl Solution.

After breakfast, duct-tape boat-building proved to be weirdly fun. Mom spread out a picnic blanket on Rick's floor and agreed to listen to the all-weather-and-traffic radio station while they debated whether the boat should resemble a rowboat or a battleship. After a few failed starts, the two of them were able to mold a thick tape wad slightly resembling a rowboat hull. Mom struggled to peel apart some tape that had gotten stuck to itself. "Okay, tape, you win," she finally said, and stood up to stretch her arms over her head. "I need to move these stiff muscles a bit. Mind if I find some music on the radio?" At that moment, the weather reporter was lamenting the summer heat.

"Sure," Rick said, engrossed in molding a figurehead.

Mom twisted the dial. A commercial urged, *"Visit the newest exhibit at the Aquarium of the Pacific, where we've welcomed a California Two-Spot Octopus to our watery* family...." Mom turned it again. *"You have to understand how the Dow Jones Industrial Average impacts..."* She adjusted it once more and got an obnoxious whine of static. "What is this, the AM radio band? Do they even play music on AM radio? I'm going to take a quick break. Maybe you can find something good to listen to." She left the room.

Rick put down his figurehead—he'd looked up the Colossus of Rhodes statue online and was trying to make an approximation of the Greek god Helios with his crown of sun rays, but he had to be honest with himself: it was not going well. He edged over to the radio and tuned in to a different station. A scratchy voice was in the middle of shouting something: *"...who cares about our city! There's an emergency SPLAT meeting on the San Fernando Road bike path next to the Metrolink train tracks. All current SPLAT members, please get down here, and bring your octopus stickers!"*

SPLAT? Stickers? Rick sat up straight. The scratchy voice continued, *"Meet past the Bledsoe Street intersection. This is Cycle-Powered Radio, spinning all the news you can use. We'll be broadcasting live at the event."*

Rick knew that bike path. It was the one his parents took him to, and it ran between the busy Metrolink train tracks on one side and busy San Fernando Road on the other. If he rode his bike down there right now, he could see what kind of hee-haws would do what they'd done to his signs. Maybe they were vandalizing something else—maybe he could catch them in the act and report them to the police.

He leapt to his feet and nearly ran into Mom, who was coming back in his room. "Mom! I think my muscles might need to stretch, too. I'm suddenly in the mood for a bike ride down to the bike path," Rick said. "I know it's hot out, so you don't have to come. It could be another test of Pre-Teen Responsibility."

"Of course I want to come," Mom said. "And if we ride together, we'll be more visible to distracted drivers. You go unlock the bikes and I'll find our helmets."

Rick hoped she'd hurry—who knew how long the SPLAT gang would be there?

SPLAT

RICK JOGGED OUT to their carport to get to work on the combination lock that held the family's three bikes to a concrete post, trying to remember if the last number was a 6 or a 4.

Mom soon followed, buckling on her helmet before handing Rick his. As soon as Rick had the bike lock loose, she pushed her iridescent blue Schwinn into the middle of the carport. "Whoops, both our tires are sort of squishy. How about you pump these babies up, Mr. Suddenly-in-the-Mood-for-a-Bike-Ride, while I go get us some water bottles."

Rick hooked up the pump and started inflating like mad. He'd gotten all four tires plump and firm by the time Mom returned with the bottles. "Thanks, great," he said, throwing his leg over the seat and pedaling before Mom could think of something else they needed before leaving.

Traffic was light since it was a Saturday. Rick thought he'd have to push Mom to ride fast enough, but instead, he found himself breathing hard behind her, standing up on his pedals to not get left behind. "C'mon, Rick. Use those lungs!" she called over her shoulder. His mom was fast for a mom. It wasn't long before they were coasting up the bike path past Bledsoe Street, where a mob of more than thirty people with bicycles were blocking the path. They stood in clumps all the way from the chain-link fence adjacent to the train tracks down to the curb of San Fernando Road. Many of them wore shocking colors of form-fitting spandex. Rick squinted in the blazing sun and saw an older gentleman with an image of a big purple octopus and the word *SPLAT* on the back of his jersey. A few others also had SPLAT shirts.

Someone driving by on San Fernando Road mashed their horn and yelled "Get a car!" at the crowd. A lady yelled back, "Get a life!" She had tattoos up and down her arms, one of which, Rick noticed, was an octopus.

"Excuse me, hello, is there an event here today?" Mom said to her.

The lady said, "It's a meeting of a bicycle group that's constantly arguing about its name. Please don't suggest a new acronym if you can help it."

The older gentleman with the big purple octopus jersey said, "S-P-L-A-T for *Start Pedaling, Lessen Automobile Traffic* is an excellent name. I don't know why our members have begun to fight me on this."

"Because SPLAT sounds like a bicyclist getting creamed by a truck! Me 'n' my crew prefer Slow Lawless Urban Growth!" shouted a short, muscular man.

A woman next to him who looked like his short,

muscular sister said, "How is SLUG better than SPLAT? Why don't you ever support me and my friends with Slow Harmful Rotten Urban Growth?"

He turned to her. "Tell me how that's any better, SHRUG instead of SLUG?"

A wild-eyed guy with wispy gray hair waved a microphone and said, "Come on over here and I'll interview you both for Cycle-Powered Radio. Let your voices be heard!" He had the same scratchy voice Rick had heard on the radio. The guy stood next to a bike with a covered trailer sprouting a ten-foot-high antenna, and he leaned to look at something under the trailer's canvas cover. "Hold on, the transmitter's running low on juice." He got on the bike and started pedaling furiously without moving forward—the bike's rear wheel wasn't sitting on the ground, but was attached to a miniature treadmill with wires snaking back into the trailer.

A voice spoke in rapid Spanish. Rick turned to see Mrs. Herrera flanked by Mila on a small bike and Dr. Herrera with Baby Daniela balanced in a baby seat that went across his handlebars. Mila wore her green Scout vest. Baby Daniela was gnawing on a chunk of watermelon rind and looked thrilled to be there.

Mom lit up at seeing the Herrera family and walked her bike over to them for the requisite hugs and kisses. "Hi, Maridol and Francisco! Are you part of this group?"

"Sí." Mrs. Herrera beamed. "How do you like my idea for our name?" She said something in Spanish that Rick didn't follow.

Dr. Herrera shook his head. "That acronym would be C-R-U-D, *mi vida*. I don't think anyone wants to be thought of as a cruddy bicyclist."

"What does this group do?" Rick asked, confused. There was no way any of the Herreras were members of a gang of vandals.

Mila said, "Today, I'm working on my Fair Play and Celebrating Community badges."

Mrs. Herrera said, "We are here to do some work with SPLAT—" She was immediately interrupted by five people who shouted out:

"Not SPLAT, SLUG!"

"SHRUG!"

"GRUNT! Go Ride Unicycles, Not Trucks!"

"FLARGLE!"

"Dude, what does FLARGLE stand for?"

"I don't know, but I like it!"

"How about Flawless Acronyms Are Really Tricky? The acronym for that would be F-A-A-R—"

Someone cut that idea off short with a "NO!"

Mrs. Herrera sighed. "Okay, we can't agree on our name, but we agree on what we want to happen: we want people in LA to get rid of their cars and ride bikes everywhere instead. We also all like our symbol, the *pulpo*." She pulled a couple of purple octopus stickers from her handlebar bag and gave one to Rick and one to his mom. "His eight tentacles show our eight plans to encourage bicycling all over our city. He's a good symbol for us: smart and fast, with tentacles working everywhere."

Rick took the octopus sticker while his stomach blorped with agitation. The tentacles on this sticker were emblazoned with tiny writing. Rick read: *Build More Bike Paths. Gas $10 Per Gallon. Free Electric Bike Shares. Public School Cycling Education. Keep Bad Car Traffic Bad.* He stopped reading.

"So you think bad traffic is . . . a good thing?" he asked.

"That's right, Rick!" Mrs. Herrera hugged him with one arm and kissed the top of his head. "Some people will only try other ways to get around when traffic becomes unbearable. Keeping car traffic bad is the only way to make it better, *comprende?*" She gave him another squeeze.

Rick shook his head and mumbled, "I don't understand." The day before, Mrs. Herrera had given him this delicious smoothie mixed with lime, papaya, and other fruits he didn't usually eat. How could someone who made such good smoothies be involved in something so wrong? Could Mrs. Herrera have been with the group that tore down the signs on Balboa?

It's not possible, said his stomach. *People who make good food are good people. Period.*

A young man wearing a bodysuit adorned with pictures of hundred-dollar bills told Rick, "With more car problems, there'll be more bike solutions."

"Simple as balancing on two wheels," said a similarly suited rider, doing just that.

Mila walked a little closer to Rick. "In Girl Scout Law, we pledge to use resources wisely and make the world a better place. With more bicycles and public transportation instead of cars, we'd have less pollution, and people's bodies would be healthier."

A bike messenger with her hair in long braids said, "Right on, sister Scout." She and Mila shared a high five.

"Who's the man with the microphone?" Mom asked, pointing to the Cycle-Powered Radio guy, who was refereeing a loud debate about acronyms among four passionate people.

Dr. Herrera was trying to wrestle the watermelon rind away from Baby Daniela so he could wipe off her chin. "That's Arlo from Cycle-Powered Radio. He's been broadcasting about bicycling on his own AM station since before the internet was invented. He does this live weekly show where he visits a different donut shop and eats and reviews each donut they make. Every cyclist I know listens to it."

"How about the man with the bullhorn?" Mom asked. The man in the octopus jersey had pulled out a bullhorn and was giving the crowd a smug smile.

"That's Mr. Platt. He asked us to meet today to discuss a new challenge we face, to show us what we can do to help. It was short notice, so not many of us could make it—this is only a small representation of our membership."

"Welcome, fellow cyclists!" Mr. Platt said. "I'm happy to say our campaign to double the gas sales tax has been successful, but as you know, we must remain ever vigilant to any threats to our goal of bicycle domination, however small. I've recently had brought to my attention some rogue road signs appearing on Balboa Boulevard, making traffic smooth where it previously was not. The signs were created by an entity known as the Colossus of Roads."

"The Colossus...," Rick said. They'd noticed his signature on the back of the signs they'd ruined.

The cyclists murmured. One of the bike messengers said, "Why can't we have a cool nickname like that? I mean, FLARGLE?"

"DOWN WITH THE COLOSSUS OF ROADS!" yelled another cyclist, waving a can of spray paint in the air. "Let's stop this irresponsible punk!"

"What? Hey! I'm not...," Rick started to say, then thought better of it.

Mr. Platt went on. "Another watchful member mentioned seeing this name on the back of signs elsewhere in the Valley. Whether this is one person or many, we don't want them making driving pleasant in areas that are already awful. I'm certain they won't be any match for all of us cyclists if we stay alert. On Balboa, I had the brilliant idea of rearranging the new signs to strangle traffic into a magnificent mess, but let's keep things simple moving forward. If we identify any more of the Colossus of Roads's traffic fixes, here's how we'll correct them."

Mr. Platt motioned to a couple of bicyclists standing at the street curb next to a pole with a SPEED LIMIT 40 sign. They attacked the innocent sign with spray paint, octopus stickers, and even some purple duct tape to obscure the words completely. When they were done, you'd never have known it was originally a speed limit sign. A few people applauded.

Mila gasped. Rick felt like his eyeballs might pop out of his skull and start flying around.

Mrs. Herrera said in a shocked voice, "That's not right. We've never vandalized anything before."

Mila pulled on her parents' hands. "Can we vote or something to stop them from doing this? It's gross." Then she turned to Rick and said, "Now we know what happened to that sign on Balboa."

One of the men in the hundred-dollar-bill bodysuits shouted at Mr. Platt, "No way, Sydney, count me out! This is one of your worst ideas!"

Mr. Platt continued talking through his bullhorn. "Remember, as you ride around our fair city and notice places where traffic is no longer as choked up as it should be, text me. We will keep fighting this fight and doing what's right!" Some people applauded, even more booed, and a couple of them chanted, "FLARGLE!" A knot of people, mostly women with cargo bikes and bike trailers, surrounded the Herreras to discuss ignoring this new plan and focusing instead on their other activities.

The other man dressed in a hundred-dollar-bill bodysuit said to the Herreras, "We're out of here. Keep the shiny side up and the rubber side down." Each of them gave Mila a fist bump.

Rick grabbed his handlebars and pushed his bike forward, straight toward Mr. Platt, who was buckling on his expensive-looking aerodynamic helmet. Rick didn't know exactly what he was going to do, but he had to do something.

"Excuse me," he said, standing on the grassy verge next to Mr. Platt.

Mr. Platt ignored him.

"Excuse me!" Rick practically yelled.

Mr. Platt looked down his nose at him and quirked an eyebrow.

"Because the Colossus has made traffic better, you plan to go and undo his work? Because you think worse car traffic will help LA? And you think *that* is doing what's *right*?"

The sun beat down on Rick's sweaty face.

"Yes, my boy. I could explain further, but I wouldn't expect a mere youngster to understand the ins and outs of transportation solutions in this car-choked city." Mr. Platt quirked his other eyebrow. "How old are you, anyway?" He was plainly one of those people who dismiss what kids have to say because they're kids.

Rick said, "Why does it matter?"

"Right on!" and "You said it!" agreed two old ladies sharing a tandem bike.

Mr. Platt patted Rick's helmet and said, "Thank you for coming out to support the cause of bicycles in LA. Trust that we will triumph in the end!" And he mounted his racing bike and pedaled down the path, shaking a can of spray paint.

Rick watched him go. He couldn't remember ever wanting to knock someone off a bike before now. His stomach burbled, *Let's set him adrift in a leaky duct-tape boat. No—let's get his address and then set up* ONE WAY *road signs all facing the same direction so he'll be stuck going in circles forever and ever.*

→ → →

After they'd pedaled home, Rick told Mom he wasn't feeling well and went to lie down. Meeting SPLAT—or whatever they wanted to call themselves—had deflated the tires of his heart. There was no way to protect his Snarl Solutions and his family's future from other people working hard with some mistaken, dreadful dream of their own.

Don't give up, Rick's stomach said to him.

"Who said anything about giving up?" Rick said, his words muffled by his pillow.

When you came into your room, you threw the Snarl Solution you made for Sepulveda Pass in the trash, his stomach pointed out.

"Yup," Rick said. "I did do that." He kept lying there. "I'll come up with something better, something invulnerable." But he didn't move.

Dad came home, and Rick heard him report bank loan information to Mom. There was a stretched-out silence. Mom eventually said, "Call the Herreras. Tell them we've decided Rick is responsible enough to be home alone after school. His last day will have to be Friday." Rick heard a rasp as she pushed her chair back. "We can tell him at dinner."

Mrs. Herrera must have picked up the phone at the Herreras' house, because Rick could hear Dad start to explain the situation to her in a falsely cheerful voice. "No, no, Maridol," he responded to some comment, "we've been very happy with you taking care of him, we just think he's old enough now to try taking care of himself."

Rick put his pillow over his head.

We did just agree you're not giving up, right? his stomach said.

"Right," he said, still not moving. But not giving up wasn't the same as knowing how to move forward.

HOW MANY ABUELITAS
ARE THERE?

AT LUNCHTIME ON Monday, Rick plunked himself in the first available seat in the cafeteria. Without cable TV, he'd resigned himself to silent lunches for the foreseeable future.

"I know you from somewhere!" the girl sitting across from him said.

Startled, he tried to paste on a smile. He didn't recognize the girl's face and tried to place where they might have met. *Doesn't matter! Say something friendly!* his stomach encouraged him. "Hi, er, I'm Rick, I'm pretty new here," he managed.

"Hey, I know!" the girl said in a loud voice. "You're part of the Girl Scout painting project! I meant to ask you, are you a Girl Scout?" The other kids sitting at the table were now looking at him with great interest.

"No," he answered. This might have been the girl who'd been so loud about her fish taco holding a bouquet of California poppies. He tried to answer quietly in the hopes that it might encourage her to do the same. "Not a Girl Scout. Just a friend to one of them."

"Okay, good to know!" she sang out. "Don't you love going there to paint? Hey, do you know Q.E.? She's doing it too! We call her Q.E. for Queen Elizabeth." She called to a girl at the next table. "Q.E., have you met Rick? He's new! He's been coming to the Girl Scout art project!"

Rick sensed that this girl made friends and assigned nicknames very easily. But she seemed genuinely nice, which would have been great if she hadn't been yelling the words *Girl Scout* and gesturing at him. He thought maybe he should bail on this conversation before the entire cafeteria noticed the words hovering over his head and decided to nickname him Girl Scout Guy. He said, "Yeah, guess I'll see you there this week. Gotta go to the bathroom now, so, er, see you." He took his untouched food and stood up.

"Sure, lunch is the best time to use the bathroom, since you don't need a special pass. I'll look for you tomorrow at the next art meeting!" she said sunnily. "Forgot to introduce myself. I'm Liz. I could be Q.E. Two, for Queen Elizabeth the Second, but I prefer Liz. I'm in Girl Scout troop six-four-five-five-six. Which troop is your friend in? Sorry, tell me later. I don't want to hold you up from heading to the bathroom."

Now Rick could see the word *bathroom* hovering around his head. He wished he hadn't said it, and wished Liz hadn't repeated it. Which was worse, Girl Scout Guy or Bathroom Boy? He noticed Tennis across the room, giving him a concerned stare. He elected not to say anything else, bobbed his head in a friendly way, and left the cafeteria.

His stomach prodded him to find a spot to eat his lunch, so he slumped against the wall outside the auditorium and ate in the shadow of some famous people exhorting him to reach higher, believe harder, and never give up on anything. He wondered if any of them remembered what it was like to be eleven years old.

→ → →

After school, Mrs. Herrera's welcome hug was extra squeezy. She said, "Your father told me you're graduating from after-school care. We are going to miss you so much! You know you can come over here anytime just to say hi, or if you need any kind of help."

"Thanks," Rick said. He knew she meant it. He joined Mila at the kitchen table while Mrs. Herrera left to put Daniela down for a nap.

"It won't be as much fun around here without you," Mila said. "Will you still be able to come to Ms. Diamond's house with me?"

"Yeah. My parents said that was okay." Rick took out his math homework and tried to care about it. Mila also had her math book open on the table, but instead of numbers, the lined paper in front of her was full of strange bicycles. It looked like she was trying to draw a unicorn on a bike on the bottom of the page.

She saw him glance at it and said, "My science teacher challenged us to sketch a bicycle from memory, and then we compared it to a real bike to see how close we got. Most of us were so wrong. Then he showed us this website where an engineer presented how mis-drawn bicycles would look in real life. They were cool and wrong at the same time. Do you want to see what I drew?"

"No thanks," Rick said curtly, his pencil scratching a hole into his assignment on dividing fractions. What was the point in solving things? You solved stuff, but there was no guarantee it'd stay solved. "I don't want to think about bikes, or about people doing things wrong." He scrawled a few more answers and shut his binder.

Mila put down her own pencil and watched him brood. She asked, "Do you want to go watch TV?"

Rick exhaled heavily. "Fine. Cartoon Network, okay?"

But when they walked into the living room, they found Abuelita there with four folks who looked close to her age. They were having a discussion in low voices. Abuelita's big ham radio with the hockey-puck knobs had been moved from the doily-covered end table to the coffee table. Abuelita waved Mila and Rick back toward the kitchen. "No *televisión* right now," she said to Mila. "My ham radio group is meeting. We'll be done in a little while."

One of the gentlemen in the group, dressed in sharply creased slacks and a black Hawaiian shirt with a pattern of pink hibiscus flowers, spoke up. "That's right, honey, the TCD has some business to discuss. We're planning our next big membership drive. You can never have too many grandmas like Abuelita here out on the streets."

"It's best we don't talk about this in front of them," Abuelita chided him.

"What're they gonna do, tell their Scout leaders about us and make sure we don't get any merit badges?" he responded.

A woman wearing a red T-shirt emblazoned with the words *My Favorite People Call Me Nana* countered, "Well, they might tell somebody, and the TCD agreed to be a secret society for a reason. You know what a pain it is to argue with nonmembers about our work. Wastes a lot of time better spent watching and driving."

"C'mon, we do what we do for Mila and Daniela and this boy here—for their whole generation." He turned to Rick and motioned him closer. "Kid, I'm gonna let you in on a little secret. You're talking to some proud members of the Traffic Calming Division. Pleased to meet ya." He stuck out his hand. Rick shook it mechanically. "We keep the streets safe for our grandkids. We all have ham radios in our houses and in our cars. TCD members around the city watch out for children from their homes, and if they see someone speeding on their street, they use the radio to put out the call, and the closest TCD member out driving gets there lickety-split and slows the speeder right down." He slapped his knee. "Fifteen miles an hour is plenty fast enough to get where you wanna go, so that's what we get 'em down to. This lady, she's a master at the brake-and-weave." He jabbed a gnarled finger at Abuelita. "She teaches super-slow driving classes at the local track."

She's teaching other people to drive slowly? How many Abuelitas are there? Rick's stomach asked.

Mila was looking at Abuelita like her grandmother had turned into a hippogriff. "This is what your ham radio group does? I thought you spent time talking about the good old days and your families."

"We do that, too," said Abuelita. "But once some of us realized how much driving talent our group had, we decided to put it to use."

"Talk about talent! She's not one to brag," one of her friends chimed in, "but she's driven in the Formula One Monaco Grand Prix."

"Formula One?" Rick said, trying to process this discussion. He couldn't possibly have heard that right. Formula One race cars were probably the fastest cars in the world.

Abuelita said, "I had a lot of adventures before Mila's mami was born."

"Yessir, we've got lots of TCD members who are Formula-One certified," the man in the Hawaiian shirt said. "And we've got a former NASCAR champ who drives an ice cream truck for us. Gotta learn to drive really fast if you want to understand how to drive really slow. And slow's the answer, my boy. Why, if only everyone who got behind the wheel of a car could never drive faster than fifteen miles an hour, the world would be a better place. A safer place. A place where our grandchildren can play stickball and bike to school and live happily ever after."

"To our grandchildren!" Another man raised his glass of seltzer in a toast.

"To our grandchildren!" the others cheered.

Rick put his hand to his forehead to keep his brains from crawling out from between his eyebrows. "So you're trying to fix traffic in Los Angeles by making everyone drive really slowly?" He hoped this was some peculiar joke that Abuelita's friends thought would be good to play on him and Mila. Sometimes older folks thought he'd like things he didn't, like hard butterscotch candies.

"You betcha. Butterscotch?" The snazzily dressed gentleman pulled a hard candy from his shirt pocket.

"No thanks," Rick said. "Mila, I need to go sit down." He turned to leave the room and Mila began to follow him.

Abuelita said, "Mila, Ricardo, respect the privacy of me and my friends. Not a word to your parents or anyone else. When you get to be a certain age, everyone wants to tell you what you can and cannot do. If we stay secret, we can focus on what we're good at, not on explaining and defending it all the time. You hear me?"

"Yes, Abuelita," said Mila.

Rick nodded, then retreated to the kitchen and collapsed into a chair. "How is this happening?" he groaned at the ceiling.

Mila sat back down in front of her unicorn drawing. "What my grandma's friends are doing?" she said. "It makes a strange kind of sense, don't you think? I mean, the way Abuelita normally drives, compared to the way she can drive when you're in the car…" She frowned. "Why do you look so upset?"

"Don't they get that they're making LA traffic worse?" Rick said, raking his fingers through his hair. His mind's eye was being assaulted with visions of his parents' delivery van trapped behind barely advancing Traffic Calming Division cars. Then he imagined those TCD grandparents leaning out their car windows to wave at bicyclists who had spray-paint cans sticking out of their jersey pockets. "Does Abuelita know about your mom and dad and SPLAT?"

As he asked the question, the gentleman with the Hawaiian shirt came into the kitchen with his empty glass. "Oh, them. Of course we know them. The bicycle loonies," he said.

Abuelita called after him, "I don't like that word, *loonies!*"

"Sorry, I know your daughter's one of them, but I call 'em as I see 'em," he responded over his shoulder. He opened the refrigerator and pulled out a bottle of seltzer. In a slightly quieter voice, he confided to Mila, "Don't know how someone who drives as well as your grandma ended up with a daughter who thinks bicycles are the answer to everything. No offense, but that's plain bananas."

Rick said, "Sure it's bananas, but how is slowing everything down any better?"

"Eh? Speak up, there. I don't hear as well as I used to," the gentleman said.

Rick said more loudly, "How is slowing things down any better? I mean, fifteen miles an hour?"

"Yes indeed, sonny, slowing everything down is better." He nodded as though Rick had agreed with him. "Fifteen miles an hour and the whole world is a happier place. Los Angeles doesn't know how lucky it is to have one of us living on almost every block. We have eyes and wheels everywhere. When we pull out in front of speeders, you can see they think, *Bad luck for me, there are so many old people in LA who don't know how to drive*—ha ha! I tell you"—he clapped Rick on the back—"it doesn't feel like work when you love what you do." He filled his glass with seltzer and went back into the living room.

Mila started to add a hoof to her drawing.

Rick stared at her. "Doesn't any of this bother you? I mean, forcing people to ignore the rules of the road and drive fifteen miles an hour, that's not the way to make life better for everyone! And forcing people to ride bicycles isn't, either!" A horrible thought occurred to him. "How many organizations like this are there?" he asked.

Mila frowned at him again. "I love my abuelita, no matter how slow or fast she is, and it looks like she and her group are happy doing what they're doing. And the things my parents and I do with the bicycle group are usually a lot of fun. We're going to ignore that Mr. Platt guy who wants to vandalize signs. Mami already started organizing a subgroup called BLAM: Bike-Loving Amazing Mamas," she said.

"The cyclists' way and the TCD's way make life impossible for drivers who need to get somewhere on time!" Rick said feverishly. How could he get Mila to understand and agree with him? He grabbed his notebook and rapidly sketched a street grid. Then he drew a couple of unicorns. "See how these unicorns are running along and they're getting where they're going?" he asked. They didn't look great, more like dogs with horns growing out of their noses, but he figured it was close enough to get his point across.

She scrunched her face a little at him but nodded.

"So now..." He added in a unicorn facing the wrong direction between them. "Here. Put in a unicorn that's not obeying the rules and it makes it harder for the other unicorns to move along properly." He drew question marks above the first unicorns' heads. "In fact, it makes the other unicorns mad, so some of them stop obeying the rules, too." He drew furious bushy eyebrows on the unicorns' faces. "Do you get it?"

Mila looked at his sketch. "The horns grow from their foreheads, not their noses."

Rick gave an agonized groan and started to erase one of the horns. She put her hand over the paper to stop him. "No, I'm sorry," she said. "I sort of get what you mean. But not everyone has to agree. Having lots of different ideas can be a good thing. You know that Muhammad Ali poster in the cafeteria that says "Different strokes for different folks"? Maybe you can relax about it a little."

"I can't relax about it. You don't understand. Traffic is a puzzle with one correct solution. And I've got to find it!"

He almost started to cry. To head the tears off, he kept talking, and was soon spilling out the story of Smotch's problems, what he'd done at Yum Num Donuts, and how he'd secretly changed the work orders at Ms. Diamond's house. Mila listened all the way through, her mouth dropping open more and more and more as he went on. She didn't say anything until he finished talking and put his head on the table. He felt less like crying and more washed-out inside after telling the whole story to someone.

"You? You're the Colossus of Roads?" Mila whispered.

"Me. I'm the Colossus," he said to the tabletop. "Me."

"Oh. Okay. Wow. I mean, I always knew you liked talking about traffic, and drawing those street things," she said. "But . . . you're going to get in trouble."

"I just want to help my family," Rick said. "This is what I can do."

"Ms. Diamond would probably make you stop if she knew. And Mami and Papi said last night they hope the Colossus—you—gets tired of what he's doing and gives up so Mr. Platt will stop insisting their group buy bulk boxes of spray paint."

Rick raised his head and said, "Don't adults want us to change the world? And persist? I mean, 'The future belongs to those who believe in the beauty of their dreams.' Even Eleanor Roosevelt thinks I shouldn't give up."

Mila shook her head. "I don't think Mrs. Roosevelt was talking about traffic, though." She squeezed both hands around her pencil. "We should tell my folks who you are, and how you're trying to help your mom and dad."

"No!" Rick said. "My parents don't want your family to know about their money troubles. Plus, what if your folks told that Mr. Platt guy about me? It needs to be a secret. Please don't tell your parents, or my parents, or Ms. Diamond, or anyone before I get the chance to prove myself."

Well, finally, it sounds like you're not actually giving up, his stomach said. *You wouldn't care about adults stopping you if you weren't going to keep trying.*

Rick continued, "I have this one huge solution I want to try out. My parents have an important meeting on Friday, and if they can't make it there on time with decent food to serve, I think that's going to be the end of everything." He laid his head on his notebook again.

He heard Mila say under her breath, "Lots of secrets in this house today." She twisted her pencil back and forth and said, "I get that you want to help your family. I won't tell anyone, but I think this should be your last one."

"Yeah," said Rick. "My last shot."

LYING DOWN IS
NOT COLOSSAL

TUESDAY AFTERNOON, RICK sat motionless on the cool tile floor at Ms. Diamond's. In front of him lay the stack of signs he'd gathered and retouched last time. Mila had dragged the signs she'd been working on next to him before going to get a palette full of colors.

"Are those signs for your huge solution?" Mila asked, sitting down next to him.

"Yeah, but...," said Rick, "I'm not sure it's going to work." Discovering that untold numbers of cyclists and grandparents were working against him had significantly increased his worry that his solution wasn't good enough.

It'll work, his stomach said. *Keep Colossusing this thing. Go on.*

His mom and dad were scheduled to meet with the movie studio people in three days, so it was either do this or do nothing.

Mila examined a SPEED LIMIT 65 in his pile. "That one could use a smidge more white, I think. You can use my paint palette, if you want."

Rick touched a brush but didn't pick it up. A heavy

weight had taken up residence on top of his shoulders. He sank down on his back and folded his arms over his chest.

No, no, his stomach said. *Lying down is not Colossal.*

Mila dabbed her brush in the red paint and kept talking. "So, I realized there's no need for centaur cement. If I spread a thick layer of paint on the big sign and press another sign on top of it before it dries, they end up stuck together. See?"

He turned his head toward her painting. She'd indeed stuck three individual dragon paintings around the edges of the big sign she'd begun decorating last time, leaving the word FREEWAY visible. Dragons in all shades of red, orange, and yellow seethed around it as if in combat. "I can make my own mythically mythtastic sign, like you said."

Rick gave her a thumbs-up.

"Want to try another masterpiece paint-off?" Mila asked. "I've got a feeling there's someplace in LA that really needs a DANGER FALLING GRYPHONS sign."

Rick tipped his head back to look up at the ceiling. "No thanks," he said. "I need to come up with a way to make my solution better somehow. Stronger. Able to convince any adults who might want to take it down, ruin it, or ignore it, that it's a great idea."

Mila kept painting. She finally said, "I wish I knew what to say to help you the way you know what to say to me."

Ms. Diamond's face appeared above Rick's. "Does someone need inspirational advice? How about this: 'It's not easy being green.' Kermit the Frog said that, and he's the wisest frog I know."

Rick didn't know how to respond.

Ms. Diamond went on, "That didn't do it? Here's another bit of advice: if you're feeling blank or overwhelmed, think of your art making a difference to someone. Because it always does. Art never stops making a difference, no matter what or where it is. That often helps me flow when I get too crunched up in my own Now-I-Must-Achieve-Great-Things thoughts. And you look a mite crunched up to me."

You are, you are crunched up, his stomach agreed. *You're acting like a pouch-bound kangaroo.*

"I'm going to help with more work orders," he said.

"When you're ready, no rush," Ms. Diamond said. "I have just a couple of them for you. The delivery man missed the last pickup, so Friday's stuff is still waiting to go." She nodded toward the stacks near her garage door, where Chompy McChompface the grizzly still sat. "Get yourself uncrunched first. Take one brushstroke and see where it leads." Someone on the other side of the room called Ms. Diamond to settle an intense debate about different shades of blue and she hurried away.

Rick continued to stare at the ceiling. A new face appeared above his: the loud girl Liz from lunch. She stood over his inert body and waved. "There you are! Hi! Is this your friend?" she said, indicating Mila. She didn't wait for an answer, but started peppering Mila with questions, introducing herself, as well as the girl she'd pointed out in the cafeteria, Q.E. Even though they all went to Eleanor Roosevelt Elementary, Liz and Q.E. were in a different troop than Mila since they were in a higher grade. Liz asked, "What's your name? Mila? That's pretty, do you use it when you autograph your work? I've been autographing my stuff *Liz the Art Whiz*."

"I use my first and last names," Mila said, pulling her dragon painting up on one side so they could peek at her neat *Mila Herrera* signature across the back.

Liz looked at the front of the painting and exclaimed, "Oooh! Let us see what you're making!" The girls gushed over the beauty of Mila's fire-breathing creations.

"How about you, Rick? What have you been working on?" Q.E. asked.

Rick waved at his own sign stack. He didn't think anything there would impress them. But then Mila showed them the SPEED LIMIT UNICORN and other signs she and Rick had come up with. Liz said, "No way. These are too funny. Can we bring our stuff over here and hang out?"

Mila nodded, and the older girls went to drag their own signs closer to Rick and Mila.

"I'm going to ask if they want to collaborate with me, since I have one more biggish sign," Mila told Rick. "Maybe you can join us? I'd like it if you did. I bet we could make something that would catch people's eyes."

That's your cue to sit up and act like a friend, his stomach said. Rick willed himself upright and stared at Mila's red dragons. He closed his eyes and pressed on them with his fingers. An image of the red dragons appeared on the inside of his eyelids in green. He opened and closed his eyes again. Red, green. Green for *go*: go paint with Mila, go fill out the Sepulveda work order. Red for *stop*: stop thinking you can help your family, stop thinking anything you do matters.

"You really believe what Ms. Diamond said, about how art matters and makes a difference?" Rick asked Mila.

"I don't think it, I know it," said Mila. "I mean, not every piece of art makes a difference to every person, but it doesn't have to. It's like this: the right art makes the right difference to the right people. Then their happy feelings start rippling along and makes other people happy, and before you know it: chain reaction. Happiness in all directions."

"Like cooperation rippling through an ant farm," Rick said. Then he felt like he'd been walloped on the head. His brain fizzed with the image of a series of road signs leading up and over Sepulveda Pass. "Wait...wait...whoa. I think I know a way to make my Snarl Solution stronger." The image in his head grew, sprouting offshoots, until Rick saw it causing a chain reaction of epic proportions. "Oh man. Not just stronger. Unstoppable, maybe."

Thank goodness. I thought you might mope forever, said his stomach.

"How?" Mila asked.

Rick stood and said, half to himself, "It's something

like setting up the most fabulous ant farm the ants of Los Angeles have ever seen so they'll never be discontented again."

Liz and Q.E. were just pulling their drop cloth next to Mila's and overheard Rick's last comment.

"Seriously, you are one interesting person," Liz said.

Mila laughed. "He really is. But let's start painting without him. He's going to go be Colossal over there for a while."

Rick skipped over to Ms. Diamond's desk. He picked up a pencil and whizzed through her two work orders, then grabbed a blank one and didn't come up for air until the unstoppable Snarl Solution idea was out of his brain and down on paper. He had to erase and rewrite segments of it a few times, examining the setup in his mind's eye. Time flew by. Finally, he nodded. This was it.

But this isn't like your normal ideas, his stomach said uncertainly. *This is really big. Everyone's going to notice it, and they'll find out it was you. What's Ms. Diamond going to think?*

As long as it gets put up and helps my parents, I don't care who finds out, Rick said. *I'll figure out how to explain it to Ms. Diamond afterward.*

His stomach gurgled, considering. *It's definitely going to make people see things a different way.*

The painting session began wrapping up, and adults trickled in to get their kids. Abuelita was one of them. The delivery guy came in through the garage door.

"Got some more purple whatchamahoosies for me?" he said to Ms. Diamond.

"You've never seen whatchamahoosies like these," she answered him. One of her arms was dripping with streaks of blue paint. "Our city's going to become the street art capital of the world. Everything's stacked up and ready to go. Let me know if you need help moving that grizzly one." She noticed her arm. "Actually, I'm a bit of a mess."

"I'll help! I'm super good at helping," Rick volunteered. He needed to stick around a few minutes longer. He was hoping most of the Girl Scouts would clear out before he left so he could privately finish a detail on one sign for Sepulveda.

"Thanks, kid," the delivery guy said. "I'll go get that furniture dolly from the shed."

"Abuelita, it's okay if I stay a little late and help, right?" Rick asked.

Abuelita said sure, and greeted Mila and her two new painting partners. "*Mi vida*, want to go get a bag of fritters while we wait for Ricardo?" She took a closer look at their new painting in progress. "Is that *unicornio* wearing a bikini?"

Mila grinned. "That one's mine."

"We've got mythical creatures enjoying a day at the beach near Santa Monica Pier," Liz said proudly. "What do you think of my Ferris wheel?"

"I did the Pegasus colts building a sand castle," said Q.E.

"Extraordinario!" Abuelita took out her phone and asked the three girls to pose next to their painting. Liz's father appeared, and he agreed that the group should take the short walk to Yum Num together. He took photos, too, and when they left, Abuelita and Liz's dad were swiping at the photos and chuckling over a sea serpent wearing sunglasses.

Ms. Diamond got busy with cleanup. While no one was paying attention to him, Rick got up close to Chompy McChompface. A faint outline of Mila's cartoony unicorns still showed underneath the dull brown boulders. Rick detached the work order attached to the sign's edge and shoved it in his pocket. He told Chompy, "You're going to be a part of this. But first, a minor alteration." He grabbed the nearest brush and some paint and did what he had to do.

When the delivery guy returned, Rick scooted around the floor, gathering everything else he needed for Sepulveda. He fastened the binder clip on top of his stack and helped the delivery guy load and balance it on the dolly, following him out to the driveway. Rick made certain his Snarl Solution signs were piled snugly together in the back of the truck. Then he helped bring out the rest of the Girl Scout signs that were ready.

The delivery guy was impressed with Rick's energy. "You've got strong arms, kid. Maybe you'll grow up to deliver things someday. I don't tell many people this, because I don't want word to get out, but it's the best job ever. One day I'm hauling uniforms, next day cupcake paintings! Never a dull moment." He waved as he started to drive away.

Abuelita walked up the driveway with Mila and a yummy-smelling bag. "Ready now, Ricardo?"

Ready to see what's in that bag! his stomach said.

"Ready for anything," he said.

Mila opened the bag and took out a warm apple fritter. "This is either to cheer you up because things didn't work or to celebrate because things went well," she said. "Is it doing one of those things?"

Rick took it from her and held it up in the air. "I hereby declare this a celebratory fritter."

He'd given it his best shot. Now he'd have to wait and see.

CUE THE HEROIC MUSIC

RICK HAD NEVER been a fingernail biter, but he nibbled with a vengeance through his Wednesday-morning classes. Would the signs get put up in time? Or at all?

You did what you could, and you ate a nice fritter, his stomach answered. *Why worry?*

There were tons of reasons why. Probably what he'd tried was too over-the-top. Probably the LADOT workers had checked with Mrs. Torres before putting the signs up and she'd yelled "Nonsense!" Maybe she'd called Ms. Diamond to complain, and Ms. Diamond would call his parents anytime now to ban him from the art project. Probably the unstoppable Snarl Solution was never going to see the light of day. Probably he should abandon all hope.

When he saw Liz enthusiastically waving him to her cafeteria table during lunch, he ducked back out and headed to the school library. He didn't want to avoid her, but he couldn't cope with her loudness and the things she might say.

In the library, he logged on to a computer to search for traffic news. The computer's firewall apparently thought live news was too intense for elementary school, so it kept redirecting him to educational websites like Kids InfoBits. He learned that Sepulveda Pass was named for the descendants of an eighteenth-century Spanish soldier. This did nothing to relax him.

At the Herreras', he kept checking the weather-and-traffic radio station. At home, he checked the online traffic maps. They all told him the same thing: the Valley was hot and dry, and traffic on the Pass was awful, as usual. He stayed up past his bedtime, listening to his radio at low volume for any late-breaking updates, but the news didn't change.

Rick forgot to set his alarm, so he overslept Thursday morning. He didn't have time to wait for his computer to load the traffic website, so he flipped on his radio while he got dressed. *Let there be good news*, his stomach complained. *I don't like it when you swallow fingernail bits.*

The news anchor told a story about the mayor visiting the new California Two-Spot Octopus exhibit at the Long Beach Aquarium, and how the octopus had escaped from its tank before the mayor could have his picture taken with it. After an ad for Taco Taco Tacos and a public service announcement admonishing listeners to conserve water, the radio continued, "Next we have Ryan Porter with the traffic report. How are things out there on the roads?"

Ryan Porter sounded dumbfounded by his own traffic report. "I have a big surprise to share with our listeners today, Linda. I had to check this seven times before I believed it, and I had the helicopter pilot confirm that I wasn't hallucinating. I'm still pinching myself to make sure this isn't a dream. Here's the scoop: everything on Sepulveda Pass is smooth going." He said it again loudly and deliberately. "SMOOTH GOING. That's right, you heard it here first: the Four-Oh-Five over the Sepulveda Pass has no accidents, slowdowns, or problems today. None. People are driving...perfectly. Gotta be a first in the history of our city, huh, Linda?"

"I'll say! Fingers crossed it'll hold up for the evening commute. And now a late-breaking update: the Long Beach Aquarium octopus was found camouflaging itself as a rock in the penguin exhibit and returned to his tank, so the mayor hopes to reschedule another photo session soon—"

Rick didn't hear what came next. He ran out of his room, karate-chopping the air and doing ninja-esque dance moves. "Mom! Dad! You need to hear this!"

He turned the radio on in the kitchen, where Mom was drinking out of her biggest coffee cup, the one that was a bowl with a handle on the side, and Dad was punching numbers into a calculator. They listened to the next traffic report together. The reporter offered the news about Sepulveda with the same dumbfounded am-I-dreaming tone of voice.

"How nice," Mom said. "Drivers getting a break first thing in the morning."

"Nice?" Rick said. "It's the best news ever! You're not going to have any problems driving tomorrow, and you're totally going to get that movie studio catering contract."

Cue the heroic music! his stomach burbled. *Start building the bronze Colossus of Roads statue!*

Dad said, "If only we could know that the traffic would be okay tomorrow, too. But there are no guarantees on the mean streets of LA."

Mom said, "Oh yes, there are. There's the guarantee that traffic will never be in your favor, no matter which direction you're going."

Rick assured her, "Mom, this is going to be the same tomorrow, don't worry."

"It would be nice to focus on the quality of my food, not the nightmare of getting the delivery van through traffic," his mom said wistfully. "Guess we'll have to keep our fingers crossed."

Rick said, "You don't need to keep anything crossed. I know it's going to be okay, because—"

"Sorry to cut you off, kiddo," Dad said, checking his watch, "but we've got to go. And you're late, so you'd better hurry up and get going, too. Hold that thought until tonight."

Mom slugged down the dregs of her coffee and she and Dad were out the door.

"Everything's going to be okay!" Rick yelled after them.

→ → →

Rick could barely sit still through the school day. He let out his bottled-up energy by sprinting to the Herreras' while his backpack bounced on his shoulder blades. Not a single dog had time to react as he rocketed by. At the Herreras', he said a quick hi to Mila and asked Mrs. Herrera if he could turn on the television to check the news.

"Homework first," Mrs. Herrera said. "And don't you want a snack?"

Of course we want a snack, his stomach chirped.

"Checking the news is sort of part of my homework," he said breathlessly. He was sure one of his teachers had assigned something today. Checking the news might have been it. "Please? It'll only take a minute." He was almost vibrating with excitement.

"Okay, as long as you're done by the time the soccer game's on," she said. "Dr. Herrera is coming home early, so we've got a date with that couch."

He dashed into the living room and grabbed the remote. The first channel showing news had what he wanted. There was a wide-angle shot of Chompy McChompface announcing THE SKY'S THE LIMIT. But Chompy looked much more interesting now. The bear's grinning grizzly snout was obscured by the SPEED LIMIT UNICORN sign Rick had stuck to it with a glop of paint.

"Ha!" Rick said. That paint really had worked like centaur cement.

The television reporter sounded like he was on the

verge of sobbing from happiness. "Today, the sky has indeed been the limit. This miraculous art installation we're calling *Magic Saves Sepulveda* has allowed today's drivers traveling southbound and northbound to experience a uniquely perfect commute." The camera cut to shots of YIELD TO HIPPOGRIFFS, SPEED LIMIT DRAGON, PHOENIXES RIGHT LANE ONLY, all the silly signs Mila and Rick had made together that he'd had installed on both sides of the freeway, interspersed with shots of hundreds of cars, none of which had their brake lights on. Then there was a split screen showing both sides of the top of the Pass. The southbound traffic enjoyed a view of the giant unicorn-faced grizzly bear waving at them. The northbound traffic got to admire Mila's churning eddy of red, orange, and yellow dragons flying above the word *Freeway*.

Rick flipped to a different channel, then another, and realized news crews from across the state were reporting on Sepulveda Pass. It was the feel-good story of the day. Every channel repeatedly showed clips of the painted signs alongside cars zooming along in perfect harmony. It looked exactly the way he'd pictured it in his head.

He wished they would show a few shots of his personal signs, the regular ones he'd ordered interspersed with the zany ones, but he understood. To most observers, the regular signs weren't newsworthy. They were ordinary objects doing their jobs. Only someone with deep traffic insight would leap to the conclusion that the zany signs grabbed drivers' attention and made them feel something other than hopeless—happy, or entertained, or at least curious. Enough drivers feeling positive meant enough drivers obeying the road signs Rick had created, which would start a rippling cascade of non-hopeless driving. *Boom!* Happiness in all directions.

Today alone, 330,000 people were going to drive swiftly through those ripples. If the signs got ruined or taken down, more than 330,000 Angelenos were going to want to know why. SPLAT would not get away with messing this up.

"What are you watching?" Mila asked. "You're humming and laughing in here." She looked at the screen and stared. "Was that my dragon sign?" She watched the next news segment without speaking. Rick let the television do the talking for him.

When the show went to a commercial, he said, "What do you think?"

"Is this the huge solution you were talking about?" Mila asked, her face exceptionally scrunched.

"Yep. That's the Colossus of Roads solution I told you I needed to do. I filled out a work order so a crew put up my signs and all our SPEED LIMIT UNICORN–type signs, plus those two big ones at the top. And it's working perfectly." It struck Rick that this story was getting so much news coverage, Ms. Diamond was bound to see it. He wondered what she'd do when she saw the big grizzly where it wasn't supposed to be. Rick was sure he'd made it easier for tons of Angelenos to "see art everywhere they look," so maybe there was a small chance she'd be pleased—or at least willing to forgive.

"You thought you could use our signs—and my sign—for Colossus-of-Roads-ing? What if you get me in trouble? Why didn't you ask me first?" Mila's voice rose. "My dragon sign wasn't even done. It wasn't ready to be hung up anywhere!"

"I thought it looked fine," Rick said. "Especially how those dragons were twisted up like they were fighting over the word *Freeway*. I think you should call it DRAGON MAYHEM FREEWAY.

Rick didn't know what to make of the expression on Mila's face. No one would be able to tell the dragon picture wasn't finished but her. Her mythical creatures were now mattering colossally to thousands of people an hour. She probably needed a minute to process all this.

Mila shook her head. "You think I should call it what? What is *that*?" The news was back on, showing the grizzly bear with the unicorn head.

"I improved that one myself. I think his new name should be Chompy McUnicornface."

Mila stared at him. Her expression definitely didn't communicate anything like Wow-Rick-look-what-you-accomplished.

"Don't you like it?" Rick asked. "Tomorrow, it's going to save my parents' business."

Mila opened and shut her mouth without saying anything.

"You're not going to sister-punch me again, are you?" he asked, half joking.

She raised her hand and he flinched. Then she said, "For your information, it's not called DRAGON MAYHEM FREEWAY, it's called DANCE OF FLAME, and it's got my name on the back, not yours!"

She waited for him to say something.

"It's the traffic-puzzle solution of the century, and you're a part of it. I never meant to make you mad," Rick said.

She narrowed her eyes. Apparently that wasn't what she'd been waiting for him to say. "I don't think it's a good idea for me to be around you right now. Abuelita? Want to go for a drive?"

She stomped out of the room.

Rick stared after her until the television caught his attention with another shot of her dragon sign.

How could such a good idea make Mila so angry? his stomach said.

"I was sure everyone would understand it once they saw it in real life," Rick murmured. He eventually turned the news off and sat at the kitchen table to attempt his homework as Baby Daniela sang her *No* song to him.

Mrs. Herrera put a plate of quesadillas next to Rick's notebook. "I couldn't help but overhear some raised voices earlier. Did you and Mila have a fight?" she asked.

Rick wrinkled his nose. "Not a fight, exactly. I upset Mila, even though I didn't mean to."

Mrs. Herrera said, "I knew something was up. She hasn't stomped out of the house like that since dealing with that group of girls who pretended to be her friends last year."

"Why would anyone do that?" Rick asked.

"Wish I knew," said Mrs. Herrera. "But she always wanted to do favors for those girls—invite them over, draw them pictures. I never liked them. They bossed her around whenever they were here. They didn't listen to Mila, talked over her. Then she found out they were handing in her drawings to the art teacher and saying they'd done them. It's not easy for my girl to speak up when she has big feelings, but she found a way to do it and told those girls she didn't want to see them anymore."

Rick could imagine how hard that must have been for Mila.

Mrs. Herrera's phone rang. She looked at the caller and sent it to voice mail. "It's BLAM, the Bike-Loving Amazing Mamas. They want to discuss adding *Papas* to the name. But BLAMP? I don't think so. Anyway, we've been so happy since you started coming over. You're a better friend than those girls ever were. The two of you get along so well without even trying. I'm sure Mila will come around."

Dr. Herrera came in through the front door and greeted them both. "Who's ready for Brazil versus England?"

"Me!" said Mrs. Herrera.

As the two adults got set up to watch their soccer

game, Rick told Baby Daniela, "Tomorrow is supposed to be my last day here. I think I fixed things so I can keep coming after school, but now...will Mila not want me here?"

Baby Daniela sang, "Meeee-laaaa."

"That's right, Meeee-laaaa. Tell Mila Rick is sorry. Saww-reee. Do you think that will help?"

Daniela looked him square in the eye and scrunched up her face just like Mila did. "No," she finally declared.

Rick sighed and picked up a cheesy triangle of quesadilla. "I'll try to think of something."

Mila still hadn't come back with Abuelita before Dad arrived to pick him up. At least telling Mom and Dad about his Snarl Solution was bound to go well.

"Dad, did you hear more on the news about Sepulveda Pass today?"

Dad nodded and waggled his head in disbelief. "It sounds like something out of a fantasy novel. I can't wait to see it with my own eyes tomorrow. Why didn't the city tell anyone this art installation was coming?" he said, unlocking the door and heading to the sink to fill a glass of water. Mom was sitting at the kitchen table.

It was time to tell them. Rick took a deep breath and said, "I'm the one who put up those signs."

"What's that?" Dad asked over the sound of the faucet. "You wish you'd put up those signs?"

Mom seemed lost in her own thoughts and didn't respond.

Rick spoke louder until Dad came back into the dining area. "No, I *did*. Well, not me exactly. Those are some of the signs Mila and I were painting as part of Ms. Diamond's project. I, er, suggested that a work crew put them there, and great things happened."

"This is something from Anna Diamond's project?" Dad said. "Now I really can't wait to see it. Do you think we could pull something up on the internet?"

"I'm sure I can," Rick said. "Want to see it, too, Mom?"

"Mm?" she said, semi-roused from the Planet of Worries. Dad helped her to her feet and they followed Rick up the stairs to his room.

He loaded one of the live news streaming sites. His parents stood behind him while he proudly played them a news segment from earlier in the day.

Dad oohed and aahed. "Didn't I tell you Anna Diamond is a street art legend? Those signs are amazing."

Mom stayed quiet. Rick wasn't sure she was even looking at the screen.

"No, Dad. The Scouts and I painted those signs," Rick said, even though the news report hadn't shown any of his signs. "Mila did the dragon one, and part of the unicorn-faced bear, and the other mythical creatures. I mostly touched up the letters and numbers so they're easy to read."

Dad said, "How nice that you and the Girl Scouts got to be a part of something historic like this. He addressed

Mom. "Sweetie, did you hear that Rick and the Girl Scouts were part of this?" He pointed to the screen as a tight shot of the galloping SPEED LIMIT UNICORN sign appeared.

Mom came back from wherever she was. "Awwww. Look at that cute thing."

No, not "Awwww!" Rick thought. *Why not "Holy shamolee!" Or "Wowee-zowee!" Or "Rick, I can't believe it, you saved our family business!"*

He said, "Well, the art's fine and all, but the best part is how great the traffic is moving, don't you think? That was because—"

"Caraway seeds!" Mom said. "I knew I was forgetting something for tomorrow!"

She headed for the door. Dad took a step back so Mom could exit the room and bumped the orange ROAD WORK sign. It fell over with a thud.

"I'm glad you feel like you made a unique contribution to this project, Roo," Dad said as he righted the sign.

"*Rick*, Dad. It's *Rick*, not *Roo*! Ugh! Maybe you should help Mom."

Dad patted Rick's shoulder hesitantly and left.

A lukewarm "oh, you played a kid-sized part in a historic event" was not the celebratory acclaim he'd been looking for. Rick paused the news playback and scrolled through the comments section. Hundreds of users had posted comments like "Love this!" and "Best commute ever!" He told himself it didn't matter that the commenters didn't know who had done it or how, as long as it was done, and that they'd probably never understand that a happy Sepulveda Pass had been brought to them by Rick Rusek, the Colossus of Roads.

His stomach chirped, *What matters is that you didn't give up. You used your talent to do something amazing, and Smotch is going to land a big contract tomorrow.*

"Right. *Right?*" Rick said. "As long as things go well tomorrow, it doesn't matter that my parents don't get what I've done, Mila's mad, and I have no idea how I'll explain it to Ms. Diamond if she ends up mad, too."

It sounded better when I said it, Rick's stomach said. *Just repeat after me: things will be fine after tomorrow.*

"Things will be fine after tomorrow," Rick repeated.

And they'll be even more fine if you can come up with something nice to do for Mila. Maybe bring her a peace offering, like an apple fritter.

How am I going to get an apple fritter? Rick asked. *But a peace offering's not a bad idea. Let's come up with something else.*

SHE COULD YELL A LOT

THE NEXT MORNING, Rick heard his folks moving around as sunrise filtered through his window. He crawled out of bed and padded into the kitchen, where Mom kept picking up her coffee mug-bowl to take a sip and then putting it down again.

"I don't need more caffeine," she told herself. "I can only control the things I can control. I am a strong woman, and I don't need more caffeine."

Dad said, "We're heading out. Your mom worries less when she's in motion. You're okay doing breakfast on your own this morning, right, Rick?"

Rick was happy to shoo them out the door. He wanted to absorb as many traffic reports as he could to assure himself that no devious cyclists or unhurried grandparents or any other traffic-mangling groups had ruined Sepulveda Pass overnight. He turned on the radio. After the first report of transcendentally smooth traffic over the Pass, he poured himself a big, celebratory bowl of cornflakes. One news segment had the mayor praising the signs as "one of the Seven Wonders of Los Angeles."

On the way to school, Rick yelled at a dog: "I did something amazing!" The dog was unimpressed. Then he tried striking up a conversation with a teacher as they both walked in through the school's double doors. "So, have you heard about how good traffic was on the Four-Oh-Five this morning?"

The teacher said, "The state of the freeways has nothing to do with me. I ride my bike to work. It's the single sane environmental choice." He began to lecture Rick about how many pounds of greenhouse gases he didn't emit while riding. Rick nodded a few times and then hurried off to homeroom.

Rick caught a glimpse of Mila headed down the fourth-grade hallway. The back of her head looked like it was still angry. He called her name, but she didn't turn around. Rick didn't know what he was going to say to her anyway.

At lunch, Rick almost sat next to Liz and Q.E., but they were playing some kind of lively game involving rhythmically lifting and slamming cups on the tabletop with some other girls.

Then he spotted Tennis. Rick slid into the seat across from him with a big smile. "How's it going?"

Tennis made a cutting gesture across his own neck. Two boys walking by the table said, "Tennis, this your new friend, Racket?" They guffawed and kept walking.

Tennis sighed when they were out of earshot. "Sorry about that. Those two are part of the group who make sure no nickname can ever truly die."

"*Racket*'s not so bad as far as names go," Rick said. "I mean, *Rick Racket*. I could be a rock star or something."

Tennis sighed again. "You have a good attitude. I know I shouldn't care so much, but I can't help it. I hate when people call me things I don't want to be called."

"I know, believe me. What is your name, anyway? I don't want to call you anything you don't want to be called," Rick said.

Tennis said, "It's Leon."

"Leon—this great thing happened and I really want to tell someone about it," Rick said, unwrapping his ham and cheese sandwich.

"I'm up for hearing about great things," Leon said as he dug into his own lunch.

Rick collected his thoughts, trying to edit his words before he said them. "Well, my parents run a business that hasn't been doing well lately, but I had an idea on how to help them out. I, um, did my idea. And I think it worked. Like, really, really well."

Leon chewed, waiting to hear more.

"So I'm happy about it," Rick finished lamely.

"That does sound like good news," Leon said. The boy next to Leon asked him how many points he thought the Lakers would beat the Denver Nuggets by in the first pre-season game. "At least thirty. They'll dominate," Leon answered him. "What do you think, Rick? Planning to watch the preseason opener?" He gave Rick a rueful mini shrug, like *we gotta do what we gotta do to fit in.*

"I sure am," Rick said. He tried to think of something else to say, switching gears from traffic celebration to basketball factoid retrieval, but his brain stuttered at the change of course.

Say "free-throw average," his stomach suggested. *Or "LeBron James."*

"You know, free-throw average. I mean, LeBron James. I mean, hope LeBron James has a high free-throw average," Rick managed.

Leon nodded. Rick didn't try to share anything else about his triumph for the rest of the day at school.

→ → →

He rang the Herreras' doorbell, and Abuelita opened the door and welcomed him in. Mila was sitting at the table. She flicked a glance at Rick and promptly stood and went upstairs.

"That girl's been in a dark mood since yesterday, Ricardo," Abuelita said. "She won't talk about it, and she said she doesn't want to go to the art project today. Maybe you can help?"

Rick said, "I'm probably not the best helper for this situation."

Abuelita overruled him. "No, you are. You're going to help." The phone rang and she held up a we're-not-done-talking finger as she answered it. "*Hola? Sí*, he's right here." She said, "It's your mother," and handed Rick the phone.

Rick took it. "Mom?"

"They loved it, Rick. They loved it!" she gushed. "One of the executives was Polish-American, and he said I cooked as well as his *babcia* from the old country! They offered us the contract!" She sounded like she was jumping up and down. "Deliveries to Burbank three days a week, every week."

He heard Dad bellow in the background, "Easy Street, here we come!"

"Yes!" Rick said. He jumped, too. "That's great news! The drive was no problem?"

"That drive! It was the opposite of a problem. It was some kind of gift. You have to tell me again which of those signs you painted. I wasn't doing the greatest job of listening yesterday."

Dad continued yelling in the background, "We're un-canceling everything, and we're going to put in an indoor pool, and buy a helicopter, and order a lifetime supply of Kit-Kats..." Mom started to laugh. Dad grabbed the phone. "We'll be home early to celebrate, so get ready for a no-holds-barred dance party. Oh, can you hand the phone to one of the Herreras? We're going to un-cancel your afternoons over there, if that's still what you want."

"It's definitely still what I want," Rick said, glancing at the staircase toward Mila's room. "If it's doable. Here's Abuelita."

He handed the phone to Abuelita, who was smiling

quizzically at him. As soon as Dad started explaining, she said, "Hey, that's good news! We were going to miss Ricardo. I'll make sure to tell the family." She hung up and looked at Rick. "Back to Mila first, though. When she gets wrapped up in a mood like this, we've got to surprise her a little. Make her unwrap a tiny bit and let in some light. Any ideas for good surprises?"

Rick's stomach suggested, *Bring on the peace offering!*

Rick said, "Well...I have something I could go home and get." He described it to Abuelita.

She said, "*Perfecto*—she won't see that coming. You go get it and I'll bring my girl downstairs."

Rick made the trip home and back. Abuelita opened the Herreras' door before he even had a chance to ring the bell. "Oh, look, it's Ricardo again! And he's got something—looks like a present. How about that? Now I've got important things to do in the living room." She winked at him as she headed out the door.

Mila sat at the table, tracing a circle on a piece of paper over and over and over. Her quiet was cactuslike, with invisible needles poking out in all directions.

Rick carefully laid his gift down with both hands across two of the table's placemats. "This is for you. It isn't one of Ms. Diamond's—I found it before we started going there."

Mila traced more circles in silence.

Rick pushed his gift closer to her. "Mila, I'm sorry. I

used your paintings to help my parents because as far as I could tell, they were the best ones. I thought you'd be happy your mythical creatures were out there for LA to see." Her circles got bigger and darker. "But the main thing is, I'm sorry, and I'll never do anything like that again, and in case I forgot to mention it, I'm sorry."

He saw Mila's eyes flick to his gift. She looked back at her circles. Then her eyes were drawn back to his gift again. How could they not be? It was corrosion-resistant engineering-grade heavy-gauge prismatic aluminum that had once warned drivers there'd be ROAD WORK NEXT 5 MILES. He'd used strips of orange and black duct tape to cover up and change letters, so it now read ART WORK: BEST IS MILA. On the swatch of tape covering the S in *Miles*, he'd sketched a rather doggish unicorn with a marker. Mila's pencil went still.

"You can peel off the tape and paint your own mythical creatures on that," Rick explained. "And when it's done, I'll help you hang it up outside anywhere you want people to admire it. I get that your art means a lot to you."

Mila didn't say anything. *I think her quiet is getting a little less prickly*, his stomach said.

Rick went on. "If this isn't enough, I had another idea. If we can go to Ms. Diamond's house today, I'm going to explain to her what I did, and why I did it, and tell her we need to get your dragon sign back so you can finish it."

Mila put her pencil down. Abuelita peeked into the

kitchen, giving Rick a questioning look and alternating between a double thumbs-up and a double thumbs-down. Rick responded with one hesitant thumb partway up.

"My oh my, would you look at the time," Abuelita said, bustling into the room and scooping her car keys out of a small ceramic dish on a table near the door. "If we don't want to be late to Ms. Diamond's house, we better leave now. C'mon, *mi vida*." She tugged Mila out of her chair. "We're going, right?"

Mila shrugged and let Abuelita pull her toward the door. Abuelita gave Rick a confident thumbs-up behind Mila's back.

➜ ➜ ➜

Mila didn't say anything or even make eye contact with Rick on the whole drive, but Rick could tell that her silence was becoming even less cactuslike with every mile. When they arrived, both a mini two-person electric car and the big delivery truck were parked in the drive-way. The delivery guy was coming out the propped-open front door with a sign-loaded dolly. "Might not want to go in there yet," he said. "Heated discussion is under way." Rick could hear shouting inside. He, Mila, and Abuelita went up the walkway and peeked around the doorframe.

Ms. Diamond and a tall woman in a scarlet suit were facing off in the center of the room, gesturing wildly and shouting over each other. The Scout leaders and girls were standing in a clump on one side of the room, uneasily pretending to check their phones or stare out the window.

The tall woman barked, "You thought hanging up on my calls would make this go away, but it won't! Why did you have to make some giant artistic statement on the Four-Oh-Five Freeway? When I signed those work orders, I never dreamed you'd decide to hang art in a place that would interfere with my job. I could get *fired* over this. A horrible lawyer named Sydney Platt called to threaten me for not commissioning the proper studies on driver distraction! What kind of an older sister are you?"

Rick realized this must be Mrs. Torres, manager of the LADOT. She was a tower of exasperated elegance.

Ms. Diamond was a colorful balloon of indignation. "The kind of older sister that would never try to get you fired! I hung up on your calls because I'm not going to listen to you yell and yell without letting me get a word in edgewise. You have to calm down and listen to me—I don't totally understand why those signs ended up where they did. But I do understand this: taking away the rest of our signs is not going to help. These children shouldn't lose out!" Rick wondered if some not-so-sisterly punches were about to be thrown.

Mila tugged at Rick's shirtsleeve. She pointed to the spot where the as-yet-unpainted signs used to be. It was empty. Barely a handful of painted aluminum rectangles were left scattered about the room, a few lonesome smiling cupcakes and palm trees.

From behind them, Liz announced, "Hello again!" at top volume, waving happily at Mila and Rick.

Ms. Diamond turned toward Liz and noticed Rick. Her face did some odd things. Rick knew she understood how those signs had ended up in a place that made her sister furious, even if she didn't know why. He mouthed *I'm sorry*.

Her face did some more odd things before she mouthed back at him, *We have to talk*. Then she put a hand to her forehead and faced Mrs. Torres. "I can't believe we're having one of our arguments in front of this many people. Can't we both take a breath and discuss this later?"

"There's nothing more to discuss," Mrs. Torres announced. "I visited Sepulveda in person and examined each sign up close. You put up not only 'artistic' signs, but regular road signs. Labeling those regular signs *The Colossus of Roads*—what was that about? Trying to show that you're better than me at everything, including traffic engineering, right? I don't have to put up with this. I'm taking the remaining signs and I'm going back to my office." She picked up a briefcase from the floor and strode toward the door, her heels click-clacking on the paint-spattered tiles.

Abuelita, Rick, and Liz all took a step backward to get out of Mrs. Torres's way. Mila took three steps forward into the house instead. Mrs. Torres clacked to a stop in front of her.

"Please don't," Mila said. "Please don't take the rest of the signs away." Mrs. Torres looked like she was waiting for the rest of Mila's speech, but that seemed to be all

Mila had to say. Abuelita came forward and wrapped her arms around her granddaughter's shoulders.

Rick's stomach said, *Look at that lady's face. I don't think two pleases are going to do it. Go help Mila. Go!*

Rick balled his hands into fists and walked forward until he was between Mrs. Torres and Mila. Ms. Diamond caught his eye, patting her hands in the air and shaking her head to say *not now*. She obviously didn't want him to reveal to Mrs. Torres that he was the one to blame for the Sepulveda art. Probably because she didn't want to see what her sister would do to an eleven-year-old.

Well, what could she do? his stomach asked.

She could yell a LOT, Rick answered.

His stomach wouldn't let him back down. *Tell her you're the one she needs to yell at. Maybe when she's done yelling, she'll realize she doesn't need to take away the signs from Mila and everyone else, only from us. She's getting ready to leave—say something now!*

Rick blurted out, "I don't always have to do what my stomach tells me to do!"

Mrs. Torres said, "Excuse me?"

Well, that broke the ice. Rick got control of his mouth and said, "You're taking the signs away because of what happened on Sepulveda Pass, aren't you?"

"Indeed I am," Mrs. Torres said, tapping one fingernail against her briefcase handle. "These signs belong to my department, and I'm not letting my sister do anything else crazy with them."

"Ms. Diamond didn't do anything crazy," Rick said. "I was the one who wrote the work order for Sepulveda Pass. Me. To help my family."

Mrs. Torres stopped tapping. "You."

Ms. Diamond gulped. Rick gulped. But he kept going. "Me. I'm the Colossus of Roads. I shouldn't have used the art, it wasn't mine to use, but I thought it would help protect my good idea. I didn't ask anyone before doing it because no one ever seems to understand what I'm talking about. So if you're going to be mad at anyone, it should be me. I never meant to cause you—or anyone—any problems." He braced himself for the yelling to begin.

It didn't. Instead, Mrs. Torres went from looking ready to yell to looking like someone who'd realized that a puzzle piece she'd been trying to fit into a puzzle came from a completely different box. "*You,*" she said again, this time as if she recognized him from somewhere. Ms. Diamond was glancing from her sister to Rick.

I think it's working! his stomach said. *Keep talking!*

Rick said to Ms. Diamond, "I'm sorry I got you in trouble with your sister, and your sister in trouble with her job."

Ms. Diamond looked at him gravely. "Art calls to us and we follow," she replied. "Sometimes it leads in unexpected directions."

He said to Mrs. Torres, "If you have to take the signs on Sepulveda down so you don't get fired, okay, but please give my friend back her dragon painting so she can finish it." He thought about what he'd said. "Actually, please, please, don't take them down. I can give you so many reasons why it's better to leave them up—traffic-solution reasons, not art reasons."

The delivery guy said, "Pardon me, pardon me," and the little cluster of people blocking the door came farther inside to let the man by with his empty dolly. "One more trip and I'm done," he said, moving toward the lonely cupcakes and palm trees.

Mrs. Torres held up her hand. "Wait," she commanded. The delivery guy waited. Mrs. Torres focused on Rick. "My assistant opens and sorts my mail for me. This week he brought me a manila folder labeled *Traffic Solutions*, without any name or contact information, which he insisted came out of the same envelope as a pile of Girl Scout thank-you cards. I was sure he'd made a mistake. Was that folder yours?"

"Always sign your work," Ms. Diamond admonished Rick, wagging her finger.

"That was mine," Rick said, remembering when he'd stuck the folder in the thank-you-card envelope about a million days ago. "I can't believe I forgot to put my contact information on it. I thought I'd be giving it to you in person. It was supposed to make you want to talk to me."

"It worked," Mrs. Torres said. "I—"

Rick's stomach made a sound like *flargle*, and he started to lose his balance. The tile floor felt as though it'd been suspended over a bed of marbles and was rolling slightly from side to side. A little tremblor. Earthquake-prone LA had them every now and again.

"Uh-oh," said the delivery guy.

"Anna?" Mrs. Torres turned and looked at Ms. Diamond. The windows rattled in their frames.

A shower of dust came down from the ceiling and Mila sneezed. Instead of the usual whooshing sizzle of car engines, a deep crunching noise approached from outside. Rick's stomach announced, *Potato chips. That sounds like a platoon of elephants charging through piles of potato chips. The extra-crispy kind.*

Mrs. Torres grabbed Rick and pulled him to the floor, covering his head and neck with her briefcase.

"What are you doing?" Rick choked out. He was vaguely aware that Abuelita had pulled Mila to the floor and wrapped her body around her granddaughter's.

"Stop, drop, and cover," Mrs. Torres said, eerily calm, and curled into a ball. "Hold on."

His stomach flargled once more, and the earthquake began.

LET THE BRAINSTORM FLOW

RICK HEARD SOMEONE shout, "Earthquake! Away from the windows! Away from anything that can fall on you!" He suddenly felt a brief moment of shaky weightlessness, as if a giant toddler had picked up Ms. Diamond's house in one unsteady hand. Rick pulled his legs into his chest.

The giant toddler threw a tantrum and started whamming the house on the ground, the way Baby Daniela sometimes purposefully slammed an empty dish against her high-chair tray. Rick heard metallic thunkings and crashings around him. This was nothing like the minor tremors he had experienced before, where all he noticed was a picture rattling in its frame or a sensation like a semitrailer had barreled down the street outside. This was clearly a Big One.

The giant toddler continued bashing its toy house around but eventually got tired and dropped it. Everything stopped moving at once. Rick heard girls crying and distant sirens, but mostly there was a thick, eerie silence. The constant *whoosh-shoosh* of traffic was gone.

Mrs. Torres told him, "Stay still. It might not be over yet. Everything is going to be okay."

"Everything is going to be okay," Rick parroted back. He stayed still. The air was thick with dust and smelled like a freshly dug hole. He heard Mila sneeze again beside them. The ground shook again, one brief jolt. Then another.

After a few minutes of stillness, Mrs. Torres peeked under the briefcase and asked Rick, "Can you move your arms? Did your head hit the floor? Or the floor hit your head?" Rick felt himself all over and said he thought he was unhurt. She addressed the room at large. "Is everyone all right? Anyone injured?"

Abuelita disentangled herself from Mila and alternated hugging her and checking her for injuries. The sounds of crying died down and were replaced by volleys of anxious questions. The Scout leaders opened up their plastic tubs with the first-aid kits inside and older girls began checking the younger kids and each other. Nothing more serious than bruises and small scrapes turned up.

The room itself was a mess. A vicious crack ran down one wall. The hanging pieces of art had fallen and splintered. Glass from one shattered window had sprayed inward and mixed with paint spilled from several cans. Every metal sculpture was upended. The double helix was now two single helices. The lollipop-holding rooster had lost all his lollipops and lay face-down, his beak impaled through someone's phone.

Rick climbed to his feet. The floor developed the marble-rolling feeling again, and Rick's stomach said, *Noooo, thank you.*

"There's no telling how long these aftershocks will go on. Let me check outside," Mrs. Torres said briskly, and ducked out the front door. She returned and addressed the room again, "C'mon, folks, let's go. We don't know how stable this ceiling is, and the front yard's clear, except for the broken art." Abuelita took Rick's and Mila's hands and steered them outside.

The street-sign condor had crashed to earth. Rick stepped around it. The metal chickens and flags once decorating the yard looked as if they'd fought a war no one had won. Distant sirens continued to howl.

In the driveway, the big delivery truck was now leaning at a drunken angle on the mini electric car. The rear of the truck was open, and road signs were strewn across the driveway. The delivery guy shuffled over to tenderly pat his truck's bumper, then started to pick up the signs. The biggest danger Rick could see was that two big palm trees had fallen across the road, blocking it in both directions. Luckily, the trees hadn't crushed anything other than bushes beneath them, but it didn't look like anyone with their car on this block was going anywhere any time soon.

A few drivers sat frozen and wide-eyed in the front seats of their unmoving cars. Others had gotten out of their cars and were walking in circles, holding their phones up to the sky. Every adult and some of the kids coming out of Ms. Diamond's house held their phones up as well, trying to get a signal. The ground outside briefly rolled on marbles the way the floor inside had, and Rick stumbled over a metal chicken part.

I want to go home, his stomach flargled.

Rick squeezed Abuelita's hand. "Can you see if your cell phone works so we can call my mom and dad? And my brothers? See if they're okay?"

She squeezed back. "The metal rooster wrecked my phone," she said. Then she exclaimed, "My radio! I can call the other radio at our house!" She pulled Mila and Rick toward her car, which was serenely resting near the curb. It didn't look like it'd moved during the earthquake. It didn't look like it even knew there'd been an earthquake. Abuelita climbed into the front seat to grab the mike from her ham radio. After a few minutes, she said with deep relief, "Mila, your mother and sister are fine! Ricardo, your parents are with them, and they're fine too. I'm going to call around and find someone from the TCD to check on Mila's Papi at the hospital and Ricardo's brothers at the university."

Rick found a fallen metal flag with rolled edges, propped up like a low bench, and plopped down on it. Mila sat next to him. The earth beneath them rode another wave, and his stomach repeated *I want to go home*.

One Scout echoed his stomach by wailing, "How are we going to get home?" This wound up triggering a bunch of Brownies to start crying. The older Scouts didn't look too far from tears, either, including Liz and Q.E., who had their arms around each other's shoulders nearby. Rick swiped at his own eyes.

Mrs. Torres kicked a metal chicken feather. "Ugh! Cell towers are probably down or jammed. I should be at city hall, directing my team to help the city. Instead, I'm here, where I can't help with anything, because I felt like I had to fight with my sister in person. I'm sorry, Anna," she said to Ms. Diamond. "I let my temper get the best of me again."

Ms. Diamond said, "You're forgiven, as always, if you'll help me get some emergency supplies from the shed." She led Mrs. Torres around the corner of the house, and the two of them returned with a battery-operated radio and packages of bottled water.

"I've got some emergency supplies of my own to share," Mrs. Torres said, depositing the water on the front stoop. She popped open her briefcase, revealing a bag of Blow Pops. She stuck two fingers in her mouth and let out a sharp whistle. "Girls! It's time for drinks and treats! Please form an orderly line to come tell me your favorite lollipop flavor!"

Rick started to stand. *Not worth it*, his stomach warned him. *More of those aftershocks are coming. Stay put.* Right on cue, the ground rode another wave. Rick plopped back down and clutched the edges of the flag with white knuckles. *The earth should not MOVE*, his stomach announced angrily. *They call it solid ground for a reason!*

Mila made no move to join the lollipop line, either. She abruptly turned to Rick and said, "You know everything's going to be fine, right? We have nothing to fear but fear itself."

She was talking to him again. Even if it was to quote a Roosevelt. He tried to smile at her. Instead of smiling back, Mila winced and wrapped her arms around her middle. *Oh, no*, Rick's stomach said, *stupid not-solid ground is giving her motion sickness too. And she's not as used to it as we are.* His stomach clenched like it was girding for battle with the next aftershock. *I'll keep myself together while you try to distract her somehow.*

Rick noticed a metal chicken foot poking out of the sandy soil and picked it up. He started to trace lines on the ground. He told Mila, "You're right. We've got nothing to fear, because we're going to get back home in no time. You know why?" The lines on the ground became Abuelita's big red car. "See these fins on the back? I've guessed Abuelita's other secret, and it's even bigger than the TCD. Those fins open up into wings, so she's going to fly us home in the Pegasus-mobile." He added blocky wings to the car, then sketched a sign advising CAUTION: LOW-FLYING GRANDMOTHERS.

Mila kept hugging her stomach.

Rick continued. "But wait, I haven't said the best part yet. Every TCD car is secretly a mythical creature-robot, and there'll be, um, four-wheel-drive dragons swooping through the sky any minute to come get us. Do you want to add one to this masterpiece?" He offered Mila the chicken foot.

She pushed it back. "You draw it." He did his best and came up with a box with legs, wheels, wings, and a snout and tail. The sign WARNING: POORLY DRAWN DRAGONS he sketched next to it coaxed a pale breath of laughter out of Mila. The sound made Rick's stomach relax a tiny bit. He started to draw the map of streets between Ms. Diamond's and their town houses, showing Mila the route they'd end up flying back home.

It didn't take long for Ms. Diamond and Mrs. Torres to distribute the water and lollipops. They started walking around along with the Scout leaders, doing their best to calm the outbreaks of crying. Mrs. Torres stopped in front of Rick. "You," she said in the same tone of voice she'd used inside. She held the portable radio, playing news at low volume, in one hand.

"Me?" Rick said. His stomach tightened again and said, *Urg. I can withstand feeling bad from aftershocks or from yelling, please not both at the same time.* "I'm really sorry you could lose your job because of what I did." He hadn't forgotten what she'd said earlier, that Mr. Platt had called to threaten her.

But Mrs. Torres remained calm. "I may have expressed myself a tad overdramatically so my sister would feel guilty. I'd like to see that whiny lawyer try to take me down." She pointed to the roads Rick had scratched in the sandy soil. "How are you doing that from memory?"

Rick said, "It's something I've always been able to do. I see a map once and I know it forever. I've pretty much memorized all the streets of LA."

"Mm-hmm. You've got some unusual neurons firing in that head. Meeting you makes some sense out of nonsense. I couldn't figure out how my sister had stumbled upon a solution to the unsolvable problem of Sepulveda Pass. Or why she'd written that Colossus name on the back of some of the signs." Ms. Diamond came up behind Mrs. Torres, and Mrs. Torres asked her sister, "Why didn't you tell me this boy was behind it all?"

"I didn't want to unleash you on him until you'd calmed down, especially when I didn't have a clue why he'd done it." She turned to Rick and said, "I wish you'd talked to me first. You said before you did this to help your family? How?"

"So they could get somewhere important on time," he said.

"Hmm." She pursed her lips. "Not because you longed to change people's lives with art?"

Rick said, "That was sort of a side effect."

Mrs. Torres held up the radio. "Art's not going to make a difference to our current situation. Based on initial news reports, the damage isn't massive, but I'm afraid it's going to be a long while before emergency crews can clear the major arteries and make it out this way." She surveyed the yard. A nearby Brownie Scout with tears running down her cheeks was holding her Scout leader's hand and repeatedly asking why her mom couldn't come pick her up right now. "I was a Girl Scout. We don't stand around waiting to be rescued. We do the rescuing." She addressed Rick. "You've proven you've got creative ideas that work. Tell me you've got an idea on how to get these girls home before dark."

Before Rick could answer, Mrs. Torres's attention was drawn to the sound of people shouting down the street. Rick looked and saw a knot of cars on the far side of the fallen palm trees, near Yum Num Donuts. It looked like too many drivers were trying to turn around or get out of parking lots, and they couldn't agree on who should move first because they'd gotten so tightly packed in.

Mrs. Torres said, "People shouldn't drive after an earthquake until they know the condition of the roads, but it's often the first thing they do, trying to get to their loved ones." She watched the altercation for a moment longer, then said, "I'm going to go straighten that out. They need someone who's prepared to yell louder than any of them."

She strode toward the knot of arguing drivers. She looked so confident, the group of shell-shocked people with signal-less phones standing in the street followed her. Rick watched her scarlet form command everyone's attention, then wave her arms like a supercharged symphony conductor, directing the drivers on how to untie their snarl and park their cars. She must have convinced them to stay put for the moment, because everyone got out of their cars to join the pedestrians. Mrs. Torres led the group into Yum Num Donuts, which appeared to still be open for business.

Abuelita got out of her car to hug Mila and then Rick. "Papi's fine. Ricardo, your brothers are fine. Your parents said they want to come here right now to get you, but I explained the roads are blocked, probably not even safe to walk. The members of the TCD are telling me there's lots more problems than these trees here: electric poles and wires down, car accidents, *ay-yi-yi*."

Mrs. Torres returned. "One traffic problem down, only eight thousand more to go."

She was trailed by a man on a bicycle pulling a trailer with a ten-foot antenna that Rick recognized as the Cycle-Powered Radio guy, who said, "'Scuse me, ma'am? I was broadcasting my donut show when everything went kablooey. First it was excellent apple fritters, then it was all 'oh no, oh no.' I saw you take control, so I said to myself, Arlo, you better follow her, she'll know what to do." He spoke into a microphone clipped to his T-shirt. "Don't touch that dial! This is Cycle-Powered Radio, trying to find a way to get you what you need. Back after this silence." He clicked the microphone off. "What can I do? I got lots of spray paint, if that helps."

Abuelita said to him, "Have we met? Does your brother Dale drive an ice cream truck?"

"Sure does. You're part of that Traffic Calming thing he does, aren't you? Since I used to drive demolition derby, he brought me to a meeting once to see if I'd join up, but moving around on four wheels hasn't been my groove for a long time, you know?"

Mrs. Torres said to Rick, "Back to your creative ideas. We've got a yard full of scared girls who want to go home, an untold number of blocked roads in our way, and no useful technology, and we're out of lollipops. If only we had more to work with."

Rick gestured helplessly. "I don't think my talent—"

Arlo interrupted. "Hey, we've got useful technology." He waved at his trailer with the antenna. "And if that lady"—he nodded toward Abuelita—"is anything like my brother, she's got a powerful ham radio in her car."

Abuelita nodded.

"Someone get me some paper and a pen," Mrs. Torres said. "I'll organize our assets and liabilities. Do we have paper and pens among our assets?" Ms. Diamond went to her shed and returned with a bin full of construction paper and markers.

Mila reached for Rick's hand so he could pull her to her feet. She looked less out of it, and Rick's stomach noticed they hadn't felt an aftershock in a while. She said, "You can bounce ideas off me if you want. Maybe if we some-how mix together all our talents, we can save the day."

"Mix us in, too," added Liz, who joined the discussion. "We won't be so freaked out if we're working to make things better." Q.E. nodded.

Rick frowned in apology. "I'm not exactly bouncy

when it comes to ideas. I just know what I want to do, and can't explain it."

"That's probably because you don't practice trying," Mila said. "Here, I'll start: if we could get your mom and dad to drive here and meet us on the other side of the fallen trees, we could go home."

Rick said, "Not happening. Abuelita said her friends reported too many clogged roads." His brain fizzed the smallest fizzle. "Hold on," he said to Abuelita. "Do you really have people from your ham radio group all around the city?"

"Yes," she confirmed.

"Can they give us details on which streets are clear and which are blocked between here and each Scout's house? If they survey it, I can put the pieces together on a map to show the safe routes."

Abuelita said, "*Sí*, I bet we can do that."

"So, step one, Abuelita and I make the maps…," Rick said slowly, trying to come up with step two.

Arlo chimed in again. "You thinking what I'm thinking? Emergency cycle-powered taxi service!" Rick had definitely not been thinking that.

Abuelita widened her eyes and clasped her hands together. "Yes, and an emergency grandparent-powered taxi service! We can work together. Come on, Ricardo, we need to get started on those maps." She hustled toward her car.

Liz threw her arms around Mila's and Q.E.'s shoulders

and said, "Let's start making a list of everyone's addresses. And organizing them by neighborhood. And telling Scouts to form teams from each neighborhood. The teams can start making construction-paper signs that say hopeful, uplifting things—and they'll duct-tape them up when they get home to let everyone in our city know they are going to be okay!" She raised her voice to an impressive volume. "SCOUTS! LINE UP!"

"Wait," said Rick, overwhelmed by the torrent of suggestions. None of them seemed likely to help. "What if no one's listening to Cycle-Powered Radio? What if the roads are too blocked? What if—"

"No," Ms. Diamond said. "Let the brainstorm flow. Different ideas build off one another, and you never know what might work."

"Just what I was thinking, Anna," said Mrs. Torres. "Let's do ALL of these things, people!" She slapped Rick on the back. "You started the ball rolling, Colossus." She used the nickname without a trace of sarcasm. "Now help it keep moving forward, whatever direction you can."

THE FUTURE BELONGS
TO THOSE WHO BELIEVE

A BROWNIE SCOUT named Bibi hopped from one foot to another outside the passenger-side window of Abuelita's car while Rick sat inside working on the map to her house. Abuelita successfully contacted TCD member after TCD member on her radio, and they told Rick which routes were clear around Yum Num Donuts and all the way to Bibi's address. With each piece of new information, Rick sketched and resketched with a blue marker on yellow construction paper and finally said, "Done."

"Gimme!" said Bibi. "I mean, please!" Rick handed her the map through the window. Bibi ran it over to Arlo, who'd set up his miniature treadmill to keep his transmitter powered up. He said into his microphone, "BLAMs and SPLATs, SLUGs and SHRUGs, the earth may have shaken us, but it's our turn to shake a leg. We got Girl Scouts here who need a ride home, and I know you're the ones to help. Any bikes able to carry passengers are needed in the vicinity of Yum Num Donuts on Balboa. The following roads in this vicinity are clear."

Abuelita put the same information out to her TCD

network, adding, "You are the best drivers in LA, and we need you! Those of you who are nearby, if you can get here safely, please come."

It didn't take long until a rickshaw bicycle with room for two passengers showed up. The cyclist helped the thrilled Bibi and her troop leader on board. Bibi wore a roll of duct tape like a bracelet and held a stack of construction paper in her lap. The top piece said EARTH-QUAKE, SHMEARTHQUAKE—LA STRONG. Off they went.

Rick and Abuelita got to work on the next address on the list Liz had given them. Once that map was done, a wide-bodied classic car pulled into the Yum Num parking lot, calling attention to itself by flashing its lights and honking its horn. Liz came to collect the map from Rick, and shepherded the girls who lived in that neighborhood toward the car. Ms. Diamond made sure the departing group had duct tape, and as they climbed into the car with another Scout leader, she urged them, "Put those signs of hope you made where your neighbors can see them when you get home—they will lift spirits!"

Abuelita said to Rick, "So, partner, how fast do you think we can make these maps?"

"I guess we're going to find out," said Rick. He focused on putting the maps in his head onto paper while more passenger-carrying bikes and TCD cars arrived to ferry girls away.

Thirty minutes or so into the process, a woman on a longtail cargo bike came blazing up the sidewalk. "Mom!"

yelled Liz. It turned out that Liz's mom, a member of the Bike-Loving Amazing Mamas, worked nearby at an In-N-Out Burger shop that was undamaged by the quake. She'd been listening to Cycle-Powered Radio, and as soon as Arlo described the safe route to Ms. Diamond's, she'd filled her cargo bike's built-in insulated compartment with cheeseburgers and fries and sprinted over.

Mila handed Rick and her grandmother Double-Doubles through the passenger window. Rick took a big bite of his. It was still hot. *We're surrounded by people having the best ideas ever!* his stomach said. *We can eat more than one of these, right?* It turned out that they could. *You know*, it continued between satisfied gurgles, *this day could have turned out a lot worse.*

The flowing brainstorm of good ideas hit its apex at dusk, after Arlo asked Abuelita if anyone in the TCD owned a truck with extreme horsepower that might be able to help move the fallen palm trees so the people who were stranded could drive home using Rick's maps. She'd put out the request, and the TCD came through. Boy, did they ever. Rick gaped at the two monster trucks with towing chains that showed up.

Every person on the street cheered as the first and then the second palm tree got dragged to the curb by neon-colored trucks decorated with flames, skulls, teeth, and horns. One was named *Grave Digger*, the other *El Toro Loco*. The delivery guy got *El Toro Loco* to come into the driveway and help pull his delivery truck upright, off the electric car. Abuelita went and talked to the drivers about clearing a few other roads so she could take Rick and Mila home as soon as they were done making maps. The monstrous vehicles roared off.

When it was time to go, Rick got out of the front seat of Abuelita's car so he could join Mila in the backseat. Mila was holding a piece of construction paper on which she'd drawn a phoenix crowing WE FALL TO RISE.

Before he clicked his seat belt into place, Mrs. Torres came to Abuelita's window and reached in to shake her hand. "Well done. You stayed calm, thought fast, and helped come up with quite the plan."

"Thank you, *señora*." Abuelita shook Mrs. Torres's hand vigorously in response. "It's so good when people listen to your ideas and say 'Yes, do it!' instead of 'How old are you, lady?'"

Mrs. Torres said, "When I meet someone who knows what they can do, I give them the space to do it. Speaking of that—Colossus?" Rick leaned forward and she passed him her business card. "I'd like to hear more about your traffic solutions under less stressful circumstances. Don't hesitate to get in touch." The card showed her work email address above the words *If you want a job done right, give it to me.* He cradled it in his hands. He'd finally gotten noticed by the right person.

Abuelita had turned the ham radio off, but the car's FM radio quietly played the news. "*Some residents are taking rescue efforts into their own hands. An octogenarian* driving an ice cream truck helped injured North Hollywood residents to the hospital, then delivered strawberry shortcake bars and rocket pops to all the doctors and nurses. Bicyclists have been seen with cans of spray paint, marking which roads are unsafe and which alternate routes are open, some adding the image of a purple octopus with alternating tentacles labeled Help and Hope." It sounded like the car-and-bike network had taken on a life of its own beyond rescuing the Scouts.

Mila made a funny muttering noise and her head leaned heavily on Rick's shoulder. He saw she'd fallen asleep.

Abuelita asked, "Want to come to our house with your parents for some food? When I told Maridol we were on our way, she said she set up the grill outside and is making cheeseburgers for the whole neighborhood."

Rick was still absorbing how everyone making space for each other's ideas had let him be part of a big solution, bigger than anything he could have come up with alone. He needed time to process. He said softly, so as not to wake Mila, "Thanks, but I want to go home and stop doing anything for a while. I don't need another cheeseburger yet."

Shush, you, his stomach reprimanded him. *Cheeseburgers forever.*

The electricity was out at Rick's house, the refrigerator had fallen over, and every bookshelf had spit its books onto the floor. Lots of things were askew, a few were broken, and Rick didn't care. Getting sandwiched in a hug from both of his parents at once was what mattered.

He helped clean things up at home and over at the Herreras' for the next day. The earthquake was measured at a 5.9 on the Richter scale, which earthquake scientists considered moderate, bordering on strong. What that meant for LA was that many things were a mess, but a mess folks could recover from.

Most of Smotch's regular clients put their deliveries on hold while they dug themselves out of their problems, but Rick's parents ended up busy anyway, getting paid by food banks and churches to supply meals. Mom's industrial kitchen was cleared by the public works department as fit for food preparation, so Rick's brothers came home while college classes were canceled to lend Mom and Dad their chopping and baking skills. Abuelita and her friends offered to make many of the deliveries. Only Rick wasn't surprised at their speed at doing so.

In the evenings, Mom and Dad brought home leftovers. Still electricity-less, the Ruseks stored the leftovers of the leftovers in a picnic cooler and played games by candlelight. Dad and Rick were an unstoppable team at Pictionary, and Mom laughed so hard when they did Mad Libs that she fell off her chair. If it hadn't been the aftermath of a disaster, it would have been nice.

After the electricity came back on in their neighborhood,

schools were closed for the week for repairs and safety tests. Eleanor Roosevelt Elementary was one of the first schools to reopen. Rick walked his normal morning route, wondering what he'd find along the way. There were piles of debris to navigate, but no sneak attacks launched by any dogs, yappy or otherwise. He hoped they'd weathered the earthquake safely. Maybe, having faced Mother Nature's power, they'd moved "attack small humans" lower on their lists of priorities.

The LA Unified School District ordered kids from districts without operational school buildings to attend the nearest open school, so Eleanor Roosevelt's entrance was pretty crowded. Passing through the double doors, Rick heard a name he didn't expect to hear.

"Carsick Rick, is that you?" One of the kids from his old magnet school was standing under the Spike Lee poster in the entrance foyer.

Rick froze.

"Sure, that's him. Hey, Carsick Rick!" said another kid from the magnet school.

Rick could hear a murmur begin: *What'd they call him? Who is that?*

Mila stood near the water fountain with a group of girls. She quietly said, "Don't call him that. His name is Rick." Rick didn't think many people heard her, but he did. Then Liz's voice rang out and dominated the foyer.

"What are you talking about? That's Rick. He's hilarious, and he knows how to do things, amazing things!"

Liz and Q.E. were part of the water-fountain group. "He helped get our Girl Scout troop home after the earthquake." The girls around Liz smiled at Rick and glared at the boys from the magnet school.

"Yeah, his name is Rick. Get it right!" Leon emerged from the crowd. "I hope he'll have room at his lunch table for me today. I want to hear about how he helped people after the earthquake."

The murmurs in the foyer were now dominated by the words *Rick* and *amazing things* and *helped people*.

Rick said to the magnet-school kids, "Hope that's clear."

"Whatever," the first kid said.

"Okay," mumbled the other. They disappeared into the throng.

Rick didn't have any trouble finding a welcoming table of kids to sit with and talk to in the cafeteria that day.

→ → →

That night, the Rusek family gathered around the television. A news tidbit showed the painted signs still set up on Sepulveda Pass. They'd weathered the disaster without any damage. Mom pointed. "Ooh! Rick helped make those signs!"

Aleks said, "Him? He can paint now? I thought everything he drew ended up looking like a dog."

Rick tried to explain. "The parts I painted...not that you can tell, really...mainly what I did was tell them where to put the signs, so traffic would flow better."

"Going over the Pass once those signs were up was the best driving experience I can remember," Dad said. "Then I had the worst driving experience I can remember right after, when the earthquake was bashing the delivery van around."

Thomas said, "Our brother, who can't stand to be in traffic, fixing traffic like a boss." He rubbed his knuckles on Rick's head. "Roo-Roo the Mighty."

"He doesn't want to be called that anymore." Mom rescued Rick from the noogie and looked him in the eye. She said, "The details about those signs still confuse me. But I get that you're amazing." She kissed the top of his head. "A nice celebrational dinner is in order. Who picked up the groceries today?" No one responded. "Oh, no." Mom put her hand over her eyes. "Don't tell me the only thing we have in this house is leftover cabbage rolls."

The phone rang at the same time Rick's stomach moaned. Dad answered. It was Mrs. Herrera. "Hello, Maridol! How are you?" He listened. "Too much food, you say. You're wondering if we'd like to join you for dinner." His face lit up. Mom shook her head, mouthing *Let's not bother them*. Dad ignored her. "Tell you what—do you need any help with the cooking part? Because I have four people here who can chop, bake, and sauté with the best." He listened again. "You'd love that? Won't take no for an answer?" Aleks and Thomas were pulling Mom off the couch and toward her shoes. "Then we won't give you no for an answer. We're coming over right now."

Things already smelled amazing when they walked through the Herreras' front door, on which Mila had taped her WE FALL TO RISE phoenix drawing. Rick's stomach burbled *SO! HAPPY!* He went to join Mila, who was sitting at the table with her sister and her father, and let the rest of his family dive into cooking tasks with Abuelita and Mrs. Herrera.

Mila stood up and beckoned him toward the stairs. "Can I show you something?"

"Sure," Rick said, following her to her room.

She opened the door and sang, "Ta-da!" The ART WORK: BEST IS MILA road sign was now nailed to her wall. "Papi helped me do that."

"Aren't you going to peel the duct tape off and paint it?"

"No, it's perfect just the way it is. It's an original Colossus of Roads piece. Who else has one of those?"

Rick very softly punched her shoulder while his stomach said *Awww*. "I feel like I still owe you a sign, though. I know—I'll email Mrs. Torres about getting you back your dragon painting. I'm going to be sending her lots of emails." Now that he knew they'd end up in her in-box instead of in some complaints recycling bin, he couldn't wait to share his ideas.

Mila shook her head. "Don't worry about asking for my sign back. I decided I'm okay with it staying where it is. My family loves it. And I know it won't be my last chance to make impressive art. Ms. Diamond called my

Scout leader to say we should be able to come back and finish our project next week. I've been getting ready." She opened a pad of paper and thumbed through it to show Rick a drawing of a Cadillac El Dorado with rainbow-colored wings and a smiley lady waving out the window.

"The future belongs to those who believe in the beauty of low-flying grandmothers," Rick said solemnly.

"No, no." Mila flipped to the next page, a drawing of a unicorn wearing a helmet on a double-pedaled bicycle riding up the 405 Freeway. She pursed her lips and raised her voice to a falsetto. "The future belongs to those who believe in the beauty of bicycling unicorns." They both cracked up.

Mila passed Rick his own pad and pencil. "Want to draw until it's time for dinner?"

"Sure." They sat in contented silence, sketching maps and myths, until their families called them to come down for the feast.

AUTHOR'S FOOD NOTE

If you visit the San Fernando Valley area of Los Angeles, you can (and should) eat burgers at In-N-Out, a nonfictional and tasty place. However, if you're looking to get an apple fritter at my fictional Yum Num Donut shop, I direct you instead to any branch of Yum Yum Donuts, or the walk-up counter at the Burbank Doughn-t Hut (*What's Missing? U*). It's open twenty-four hours a day.

Also, if you get the chance to eat Polish food, try a cabbage roll—known in Polish as *Gołąbki* (pronounced "go-wump-ki"). They are super delicious.

AUTHOR'S ROAD SIGN NOTE

Before the 1920s, road signs came in more colors than today, including green, red, yellow, blue, purple, black, even silver. They were produced in different shapes and sizes too. I wonder if any early drivers admired them as art.

Rick and Mila aren't the only ones to see the potential for art and good deeds in modern road signs. An artist named Clet Abraham uses stickers to turn road signs in Florence, Italy, into comical cartoons. Another artist, Richard Ankrom, secretly made part of the 110 Freeway in Los Angeles safer by painting his own giant freeway sign.

Since writing this story, I've been seeing art everywhere I look when I travel the roads. Keep your eyes peeled. Maybe you will too.

ACKNOWLEDGMENTS

Big, warm hugs of gratitude to the following talented people:

My editor, Margaret Ferguson, and every wonderful person at Holiday House.

My agent, Ammi-Joan Paquette, and the longing pangolins of EMLA.

My family members, who insist I'm doing a good job even when I won't let them read anything I'm writing. A special thanks to my mom and dad, who've fed me good Polish food my whole life. I'm lucky you're my parents for so many reasons. Your ability to hand-sell my books is second to none.

My steadfast friends, some of whom lent me their names for characters (especially Maridol Linares, whose unique first name came from combining her grandmother Maria Dolores' two names), and some of whom lent me their houses as writing retreats while they kindly went on vacation (or kindly ignored me in the basement). This is what I was doing that whole time. Plus napping.

My fabulous readers, who take the time to let me know they care about my stories. You are the reason I write.

A salute to the LADOT for making LA streets function as well as they can, and to the LA County Bicycle Coalition, who showed me how to carve out a car-free existence in the city.

A sincere apology to the Traffic Calming Division for blowing your cover—maybe you can stop pulling out in front of me when I really need to get somewhere? Please?